Exceptional Women Environmentalists

Exceptional WOMEN Environmentalists

Frances Rooney

Second Story Press

Library and Archives Canada Cataloguing in Publication

Rooney, Frances
Exceptional women environmentalists / by Frances Rooney.

(Women's hall of fame series)
Includes bibliographical references.
ISBN 978-1-897187-22-7

1. Women environmentalists—Biography—Juvenile literature.
I. Title. II. Series.

GE55.R66 2007 j363.7'0092 C2007-904602-9

First published in the USA in 2008
Second printing 2010

Edited by Kathleen J. Brooks
Designed by Melissa Kaita

Printed and bound in Canada
Printed on 100% post-consumer reycled paper

Second Story Press gratefully acknowledges the support of the Ontario Arts Council and the Canada Council for the Arts for our publishing program. We acknowledge the financial support of the Government of Canada through the Book Publishing Industry Development Program.

Canada Council for the Arts Conseil des Arts du Canada

Published by
Second Story Press
20 Maud Street, Suite 401
Toronto, ON
M5V 2M5
www.secondstorypress.ca

The author may be reached at frooney2002@yahoo.com

Contents

To Harry Thurston,
who when I was ten, introduced me
to the fascination of ecology
and to Deanna Katharina Derksen

Introduction

Global warming. Starving animals. Dying forests. Poisoned rivers. Farmland turned into desert. Ancient trees clear-cut. Governments and corporations interested only in making money. The entire planet in danger of becoming a toxic, lifeless rock.

If we want to prevent disasters that make Hurricane Katrina look like a minor event, if we want to keep every living thing on this planet from being poisoned, if we want a planet to live on, we must act now. Who cares?

Millions of us care. Millions of us are doing what we can, day to day, to help. We are reducing, reusing, recycling, some of us in a casual way, others with more enthusiasm. And everywhere, people who have dedicated their lives to our environment are doing astonishing things. With almost unbelievable courage and passion, these people are working to stop the damage. They are saying, "Enough."

When I started researching this book, I wondered how I would find ten women who are exceptional environmentalists. The difficulty quickly became how to choose among all these incredible activists.

Exceptional women environmentalists everywhere share courage, enthusiasm, energy, and excitement. Many of them share hope. They all recognize that individuals can achieve tremendous things — and that groups can do more. Whatever the focus of their work, certain themes keep coming up: global warming is the greatest single danger; biodiversity is crucial; at all levels, life is lived in relationships; women's rights are central to environmental health; hope is essential to being able to carry on.

Being an environmentalist is not easy. Rachel Carson died of a disease that may have been the result of environmental poisons. Many of the women in this book have received death threats. Dai Qing has been imprisoned. Olya Melen has been accused of being a spy and a traitor. Fatima Jibrell lives in a war zone. Marina Silva has massive heavy-metal poisoning.

And still they go on. The ten here are the tip of the iceberg. Other Canadians include Ruby Dunstan, Maude Barlow, Josephine Mandamin, Rosalie Bertell, Ursula Franklin, Biruté Galdikas, Elizabeth May, Lydia Dotto, and Sharon Butala. Then there are Tokiko Kato of Japan, Molly Gaskin of Trinidad and Tobago, and Laila Iskandar Kamel of Egypt, who serve on the UN Environmental Program. Wangari Maathai of Kenya, who won the 2004 Nobel Peace Prize (see her story in *Great Women Leaders*, also in this series), founded Africa's Green Belt Movement. Anne Kajir leads the campaign for forests and sustainable development in Papua New Guinea. Michiko Ishimure of Japan helped bring toxic chemical poisoning to the attention of the world with her discoveries about Minamata disease. Kris Tompkins raises money, buys, and donates huge pieces of land for public parklands in Patagonia. Masumeh Ebtekar is vice president and environmental minister of Iran. Gro Harlem Brundtland has worked for decades to protect the environment as a cabinet minister and prime minister of Norway before becoming Director-General of the World Health

Organization. Thousands more women work with environmental organizations as paid staff and volunteers. An e-mail or phone call to any of these groups opens a whole new world — one that you might want to be part of.

Finally, there are the millions, perhaps billions, of us, who daily try to do our part. We learn from prominent environmentalists, from our mothers and grandmothers, and from each other. Women of all cultures and all kinds of ways of living have practiced care and conservation — have been environmentalists — for centuries. We need to act in whatever ways we can, in public or private. We come to the work from many places: as activists, poets, teachers, parents, bankers, politicians, filmmakers, people who refuse to buy a product because the plastic packaging it comes in harms the earth. Like the women in this book, we all need to act out of the knowledge that we are part of something far bigger than we are, to honor the life in and around us, and to walk gently on our planet.

—Frances Rooney

We do not inherit the earth from our parents, we borrow it from our children.

—First Nations saying

Rachel Carson

1907-1964

The Eloquent Voice of Warning

From the time she was a child, Rachel Carson had two passions: writing and the sea. When these passions combined with what she named her boundless sense of wonder, she dramatically changed the world and how we live in it. Rachel Carson is considered the founder of the modern environmental movement.

Rachel was born on a farm in Springdale, Pennsylvania, when her sister Marian was ten and brother Robert was eight. Her mother, Maria Carson, taught piano lessons for fifty cents an hour, and her father, also Robert, worked in the local electrical station and real estate office. Two things in Rachel's happy childhood stood out for her: lots of pet dogs and cats and long walks with her mother. On those walks they looked at, listened to, felt, and smelled the flowers and trees, animals, insects and birds, and the sky, with its planets, moons, stars, comets, and asteroids. She also discovered a love of reading and a deep love of the sea, even though she lived far from it and had never seen it.

Rachel Carson as a child, reading to her dog, Candy

Rachel began writing stories when she was very young, and bound them into small books from the time she was ten. Her brother had enlisted in the army when the United States entered World War I in 1917, and his letters home included many stories about his and his friends' struggles in the trenches in France. When one story about a friend of Robert's made a particularly deep impression on Rachel, she used that story as the basis of one she wrote herself. She sent the story to *St. Nicholas*, a leading magazine for young readers. Not only did the magazine publish Rachel's story, but she also won a prize for it: $10. *St. Nicholas* published two more of her stories and paid her for them. At eleven, Rachel Carson was a professional writer.

Rachel adored school, and when her eagerness to study and learn became clear, Maria Carson decided to make sure that her daughter got all the education she wanted. The family had little money, so in order to go to college, Rachel needed to win a scholarship. She worked very hard, got that scholarship, and in 1925 enrolled at the Pennsylvania College for Women.

No one was surprised when Rachel decided to study English literature in university. For the first three years, she wrote essays and stories for her courses and the school newspaper. But then, in her third year, she took a required biology course. Mary Skinker, who taught the course, was well known for her ability to fascinate students. Rachel became so entirely intrigued that she decided to change her major subject. In the summer between her third and fourth years she did make-up courses, and in her fourth year she took extra courses to complete the requirements for a degree in science. In May 1929, she graduated with high honors.

It was not an easy time for the Carsons. Rachel's sister Marian was ill from diabetes, which was then a fatal disease. Marian and her two daughters had moved back home just when Rachel's father's ability to earn money decreased. To

keep everyone together, Maria sold some of the family's most treasured possessions and Rachel tutored students.

Meanwhile, Mary Skinker had gone to teach at Johns Hopkins University in Baltimore, Maryland. Mary encouraged Rachel to do a master's degree there. Although she had little hope of being able to pay her way, Rachel applied, was accepted, and received a $200 scholarship. It was a beginning. That summer, she won a fellowship to work in marine biology at the Woods Hole Oceanographic Institution off Cape Cod. Not only would this job bring in more money but it also meant that for the first time, Rachel, who had loved the sea from a distance all her life, would work with its creatures and would live beside it.

She also went to the U.S. Bureau of Fisheries in Washington to check out what kind of work she might be able to get there. She was told that they did not hire women who were scientists, but to check back when she had finished her studies. Maybe there would be some kind of job she could do.

In October 1929 the stock market crashed and the Great Depression began. Rachel's father was able to find some work doing odd jobs, but Rachel had to provide the main family income. She rented a house outside Baltimore for her mother and father, sister, two nieces, brother, and herself. For the next three years she studied full time, which meant classes and labs for forty hours a week. She also worked in the labs as an assistant, taught half time at the University of Maryland, and taught every summer. She graduated with a master's degree in 1932 and taught full time for another three years.

Rachel's father died in 1935. Marian was extremely ill, and their brother had moved away. Rachel went back to the Bureau of Fisheries looking for a job. The Bureau had not changed its policy about hiring women scientists, but as she was leaving the interview, Elmer Higgins, with whom she had met in 1929, asked her if she could write. A door was opening.

The Bureau was creating several seven-minute radio programs called "Romance Under the Waters." The programs so far had been dull and lifeless. They weren't working. Could Rachel do better? She could and did. She was still teaching and wrote the shows at night after work. Her pay was $19.25 a week.

The first time that Rachel Carson went to the U.S. Bureau of Fisheries to look into job possibilities, she was told that there were no jobs for women scientists. Her interviewer told her, "Teach school, my dear."

The next year, 1936, Marian died of pneumonia and complications from diabetes. Rachel and her mother decided to raise Marian's two girls. Maria ran the house, Rachel brought in the money.

That same year, a job came up for a junior aquatic biologist. The competition involved an exam. The person with the highest score would get the job. Thousands of men and four women wrote the exam. Rachel won the competition, got the job, and went to work full time at the Bureau of Fisheries. Her pay went up to $28.48 a week. She stopped teaching, but continued with the radio programs and writing feature articles on fishing for the *Baltimore Sunday Sun.*

When the broadcasts ended, Rachel began work on a series of pamphlets on sea creatures. The Bureau decided to collect several of these pamphlets in a book, and Elmer Higgins asked Rachel to write an introduction for it. She stayed up writing most of that night, and the next day went in to the office with twenty-five pages. Higgins told her that they couldn't use her essay, that it was too beautiful to use as a book introduction, and suggested that she send it to the prestigious *Atlantic Monthly*. In September 1937, the magazine published "Undersea" and paid Rachel $75, a huge fee at the time.

Rachel Carson with wildlife artist Bob Hines checking specimens for her book, *The Edge of the Sea,* in the early 1950s

From that story came Rachel's first book, *Under the Sea Wind*, which she wrote at the rate of two pages each night over three years. It was published in November 1941. The timing was disastrous. On December 7, Japan bombed Pearl Harbor and the United States entered World War II. The book received good reviews, but since the war was dominating everyone's thoughts, it sold few copies.

However, with the war in the Pacific and across the Atlantic in Europe, suddenly the sea and its coastlines became of huge importance to the government. Also, with the need to feed all the troops overseas, food — particularly meat — was less available, and it grew necessary to try to use more fish in people's diets at home. Rachel read everything she could get her hands on about the sea: government reports, literature, scientific documents.

During this research, Rachel began to find reports of a pesticide that was being sprayed onto crops, forests, and even onto soldiers to get rid of lice. Reports sometimes included notes that Dichloro-Diphenyl-Trichloroethane (DDT), then believed to be an almost miraculous insecticide, was killing birds and animals as well as insect pests. Its impact on humans was not known, and yet soldiers were being sprayed so heavily with the white powder that they had to rub it off their faces and hands and out of their eyes. Quietly, Rachel began to collect information on this insecticide.

Meanwhile, she was promoted at work. Life was busy there and at home, but things grew easier and home life was happy. Rachel loved the earth and the life that sprang from it, and although humans were doing damaging things,

In 1963, the United States used 900,000 pounds (400 million kg) of pesticides. Current usage is four times that amount, and the U.S. still exports DDT overseas.

she and everyone else firmly believed in the planet's ability to recover from our mistakes.

When the atom bomb was dropped at the end of World War II, that belief changed. Rachel Carson and other thoughtful people came to realize that for the first time in history, humans had the ability to destroy all the life on our planet and perhaps the planet itself. It was a horrifying discovery.

In 1948, still writing after work, Rachel started another book. As with earlier publications, Maria, now eighty-one years old, typed for her daughter. Rachel's friends thought her new book might sell a few copies but that it would never make much impact.

The Sea Around Us came out in July 1951. It went immediately to the *New York Times* Best Seller List and stayed there for eighty-six weeks. For thirty-nine of those weeks it was number one. The publisher needed so many copies that it had to hire two companies to print the book at the same time. People were fascinated by the huge amount of information and by the way Rachel told the story of the sea. One reviewer was so impressed that he insisted Rachel must really be a man! The work was translated into more than thirty languages and sold millions of copies worldwide. And as people read it, their sense of the world and our place in it began to shift. *The Sea Around Us* is still for sale in bookstores.

Meanwhile, Rachel had started to raise money to buy land for a conservation area near the house she had recently purchased on the coast of Maine. She was in demand as a speaker, won many awards for her book, and in 1952 received three honorary doctorate degrees. Her influence and her message were spreading. And finally she was financially secure enough to quit her job and write full time.

Her next book was *The Edge of the Sea*, about the life and activity of the shoreline. It, too, went straight to the best seller list. Parts of it appeared in many magazines, and Rachel's

work received still more awards.

Rachel's three-part series of excerpts from *The Sea Around Us* in the *New Yorker* magazine in 1949 paid her almost an entire year's salary.

By the late 1950s, more than two hundred new "magic killing chemicals" were being manufactured and used in huge quantities. No one knew what these chemicals were doing to plants, animals, insects, the air, the water, and people. Scientific reports indicated that chemicals that were intended to kill insect pests were in fact killing all kinds of other living things. And, through genetic mutation, these insecticides were encouraging the development of new and tougher kinds of insects that

The Rachel Carson National Wildlife Refuge in Maine

Rachel Carson wrote in her 1956 article in *Women's Home Companion*, "Help Your Child To Wonder," that the greatest gift a person can have, a sense of wonder about the natural world, is also the most powerful tool for getting people to protect and preserve our planet. In 1965, after her death, her friends combined the article with photographs and turned it into the book, *The Sense of Wonder*.

the poisons could not kill. It was also becoming clear that these chemicals were interrupting the food chain (the way that nature maintains balance in the world by the patterns of who eats what), and that some were causing cancer. Meanwhile, government and the manufacturers of these chemicals were advertising them as miracle cures for crop problems and food shortages. Rachel decided that she had to do something.

She tried to sell articles to various magazines, articles warning of this danger. She was called an alarmist, a silly woman, a troublemaker. No one would publish anything so frightening. In 1958, Rachel took the material she'd been collecting for years and began adding to it, doing in-depth research for another book. That December her mother died, and she lost her beloved lifelong companion. After a short break, she went back to work. She consulted more than a thousand sources and wrote to and spoke with scientists all over the United States. Some scientists were too afraid to communicate with her. Others wrote to her anonymously, fearing that they would lose their jobs. All the while, the government and the manufacturers praised and advertised their wonderful chemicals.

Silent Spring was published in 1962, after four years of research and writing. It went straight to the top of the best seller

lists. At the same time, chemical companies called Rachel a nut, a nosy biddy, and a fanatic. They spent hundreds of thousands of dollars advertising their chemicals and trying to find loopholes in Rachel's research. CBS Television did an hour-long program on the book. And through it all, Rachel remained calm. She knew that her research could not be undermined and that what she had discovered was true: that if we do not stop using all these chemicals, we will kill all living things on our planet, including ourselves. We will have created the silent spring before the dead summer, a time when no birds sing, no trees or flowers grow. There will be no good food to eat, no good air to breathe, no water that is not poisonous.

While she was writing *Silent Spring*, Rachel started to get tired easily. Although she told no one for some time, she had breast cancer. One of Marian's daughters had died, leaving a nine-year-old son, Roger, whom Rachel had adopted. She arranged for friends to raise Roger after she died, then spent as much time as she could at her cabin in Maine with him and with her friends Dorothy and Stanley Freeman. Rachel Carson, founder of the modern environmental movement, died on April 14, 1964. She was fifty-six.

Rachel Carson had not been optimistic that the use of pesticides would decrease. She was right. In the 1990s, the world used eight billion pounds (3.6 billion kilograms) of pesticides, four times the amount used in 1963. DDT, while restricted in the U.S. and Canada, is still produced and sent to countries all over the world. Nonetheless, her work made a huge difference by giving us a new perspective on our planet and how we use and abuse it. In her lifetime and since then, the world has acknowledged her contribution. Her campaigns led U.S. President John F. Kennedy to establish that country's Environmental Protection Agency. The U.S. also issued a stamp in her honor. The wildlife refuge she started has grown until it now extends for many miles along the coast of Maine.

Pennsylvania has a holiday in her honor. In 1980, sixteen years after her death, Jimmy Carter presented the Presidential Medal of Freedom, the highest honor given to civilians in the United States, to her nephew Roger in her honor. At the ceremony, President Carter said:

> "Never silent herself in the face of destructive trends, Rachel Carson fed a spring of awareness across America and beyond. A biologist with a gentle, clear voice, she welcomed her audiences to her love of the sea, while with an equally clear determined voice she warned...of the dangers human beings themselves pose for their own environment. Always concerned, always eloquent, she created a tide of environmental consciousness that has not ebbed."

Jane Goodall

1934 -

Turning Compassion into Action

Sometimes things that happen in a person's early life seem to set the stage for what that person will do later. Three of these kinds of events stand out for Jane Goodall. The first happened when she was four and was given a tiny stuffed-toy chimpanzee. As a child she carried it everywhere. She still has that toy; now it sits on her dresser in England. Then, not long after she received the chimp, her mother took her to visit friends on their farm. The chickens there fascinated her: how could a bird that small make an egg so big? And where did it come out? The adults around her didn't satisfy her curiosity,

so she snuck out to the chicken coop early one morning to find out for herself. That discovery was one of the most exciting moments of her young life. The third event was a dream she had throughout her childhood of living like Tarzan or Dr. Doolittle. Looking back, it is not surprising that she has spent more than fifty years studying animal life, specifically chimpanzees, and for the most part, in the jungles of Africa.

Jane was born in London, England. Her mother, Vanne Goodall, was a successful author, who encouraged Jane to do whatever she wanted with her life, and to be dedicated and insightful. Neither of them let the fact that Jane has prosopagnosia — a disease that keeps her from recognizing faces — get in the way. "My mother used to tell me, 'Jane, if you really want something, you work hard enough, you take advantage of opportunities, you never give up, you'll find a way.'"

Jane's parents divorced when she was eight, and she and her mother moved to Bournemouth to live with three more strong women: Jane's grandmother and two great aunts. Jane still lives in that house part of each year.

When she finished high school, Jane trained to be a secretary and got a job at Oxford University. To finance the travel she desired, Jane worked at a second secretarial job with a company that made documentary films. The money she made at that job paid for her first trip to Africa.

By the time Jane was twenty-three, she was in Kenya, where she found work in Nairobi. She heard about the husband-and-wife team of Mary and Louis Leakey, who were studying apes in the wild, not far from Nairobi. She went to see them. Impressed by her enthusiasm for the natural world and its inhabitants and by her skills as a secretary, the Leakeys hired her to work at the Gombe Stream Research Centre in Gombe National Park, Tanganyika (now Tanzania).

In 1960, Louis Leakey was looking for someone who could go into the wild and study chimpanzees in their natural

surroundings. This person needed to be calm, patient, observant, and able to record complicated and detailed findings. The ideal person would also be someone who could observe without making assumptions about what the chimps were doing and how they were acting. Someone with no scientific training would be perfect. Leakey asked Jane if she would be interested. The project would be a long one, lasting perhaps ten years. Jane thought it over, decided that three years was more likely, and accepted the position. This would turn out to be the beginning of the longest research study ever undertaken of animals in the wild. The study is still going on.

But when Louis Leakey first approached Jane Goodall, it was not at all certain that the project would even get off the ground. Convincing the British authorities to allow a young woman to go into the wild on her own was not easy. Only when her mother offered to spend the first three months with Jane did they agree to allow her to go. Almost no one believed that Jane would last to the end of those three months. Many people said that she wouldn't even last three weeks.

Those first three months, July, August, and September, were discouraging. Jane could spot chimpanzees from

Jane Goodall was one of three women scientists known as "Leakey's Angels." The others were American Dian Fossey, who studied gorillas in Rwanda until her murder on December 27, 1985, and German-born Canadian, Biruté Galdikas, who studies orangutans in Borneo and now also teaches at Simon Fraser University, is *professeur extraordinaire* at Indonesia's Universitas Nasional in Jakarta, and is president of Orangutan Foundation International, which is based in Los Angeles, California.

a distance, but could never get close enough to them to distinguish one from another, or to observe their behavior. Within weeks, she and her mother both got malaria. Her mother went for treatment, but Jane refused to leave her work and struggled along, even though she was ill. She finally recovered, but then came down with malaria again. And still the chimps were too far away to observe.

Then one day a large male approached their camp and began to screech and bounce around. Jane eventually figured out that he wanted a banana that was just inside the tent. That banana — and many bananas after it — made all the difference. Jane and the chimps started to become friends. As that happened, Jane began the observations that have made her famous and that have changed the way humans see our relationship to other animals. (And oddly enough, her memory problem with faces did not extend to the chimpanzees. She had no problem recognizing each of them individually.)

The fact that humans make tools, and use them for specific purposes, had always been considered the great divide between us and the rest of the animal world. By October, just three months into her research, Jane had discovered evidence that humans are not the only toolmakers. She had seen a chimpanzee pull a stick from a tree, tear off the leaves, make a pointed end, and use the stick to dig termites out of their nest. This observation shattered one of the most basic assumptions about the difference between humans and animals.

Over time, Jane recorded many other surprising findings. For example, chimpanzees eat meat, not just vegetation and insects. They make plans that show they are aware of actions and consequences. They can experience awe. They sometimes go to war. Females adopt orphaned infants. They use certain plants for medicine, including the aspilia plant, which seems to relieve stomach aches or to decrease internal parasites. And chimps use many different types of sounds to speak a kind

of language. Eventually it was discovered that humans and chimpanzees share 98 percent of the same DNA.

Although these findings no longer surprise us, before Jane Goodall's work, no one in the Western world knew that primates other than humans possessed any of these characteristics. Scientists did not believe that animals have personalities and emotions. Nor did anyone realize that those primates closest to us in development can do many of the same things we do. Jane's research showed us just how closely related we are to the other animals of the earth, and to the planet we all share. Her work makes us realize that we have no right to use other animals, or the earth, in abusive ways.

Louis Leakey realized that Jane's sophisticated and groundbreaking findings put her in a position where university study would both enrich her research and give her more status in the scientific community. He asked her to go back to England to do a doctorate in ethology — the study of animal behavior, particularly in the wild. She had no desire to leave her work, or to study, but nevertheless agreed to go. She completed her studies at Cambridge University in 1965 and became one of only eight people to earn a PhD without first having completed a bachelor's degree.

Jane married Dutch photographer Hugo van Lawick in 1964 and had a son, Hugo, fondly known as "Grub." Back in Gombe, she wrote or did research in the mornings and spent afternoons with her son. Following a divorce in 1974, she remarried. Her second husband, Derek Bryceson, was a member of the Tanzanian parliament and head of the country's national park system. The couple was together until his death in 1980.

Almost from the start of her work in Africa, Jane had realized that chimpanzees and other species were in danger. When she began her observations in 1960, it was estimated that there were two million chimpanzees across Africa. By 2005,

Jane Goodall with a young chimpanzee

that figure had plunged to 125,000. Very early in her work, Jane began her campaign of speeches and writings to make people aware of the threat we humans are to the animals of our planet.

> "Chimpanzees have given me so much. The long hours spent with them in the forest have enriched my life beyond measure. What I have learned from them has shaped my understanding of human behavior, of our place in nature."
>
> —Jane Goodall

In 1977, she founded the Jane Goodall Institute, which emphasizes the power of individuals to make a difference for all living things, and offers programs in conservation, education, and outreach. She also founded the Chimpanzee Guardian Project in Tanzania, which fights to save chimpanzees and their habitat. Jane has written more than thirty books and has traveled tirelessly around the world. Since 1964, the National Geographic Society has been a huge and influential promoter of her work; it has published more articles about her and used her picture on more covers than it has of anyone else. She has also been featured in numerous videos, DVDs, and television specials.

In 1991, Jane founded the grassroots organization Roots and Shoots, which has grown to more than eight thousand groups in one hundred countries. She got the idea for Roots and Shoots after meeting a group of middle school students who were eager to learn about her work, and about how they could help the planet and its living things. Jane understands that knowledge leads to compassion and that compassion leads to action. She also knows that people acting together are stronger than individuals working alone. Through Roots and Shoots, people around the world connect and share information, news, and thoughts about how they can act on global issues — such as helping endangered species. These people can then work on universal issues from their own country or town while at the same time getting to know others from around the world.

Jane Goodall has received many awards in recognition of her work as a scientist, an advocate of peace, and a leader in bringing environmental issues to people's attention. These awards include: Japan's Kyoto Prize for scientific research, the Medal of Tanzania, the Benjamin Franklin Medal in Life Science (in the U.S.), the Gandhi-King Award for Nonviolence, the Animal Welfare Institute's Albert Schweitzer Award, the Commander of the British Empire (CBE), and the National Geographic Hubbard Medal "for her extraordinary study of wild chimpanzees and for tirelessly defending the natural world we share."

For the last few years Jane has divided her time among her work in Gombe, and her homes in England and in Dar es Salaam, Tanzania. In her worldwide advocacy, she gives talks and meets with members of Roots and Shoots. She continues to be the Director of Research at the Gombe Centre, a position she has held since 1967. The Chimpanzee Guardian Project, which she founded, is in Tanzania as well, fighting to save chimpanzees and their habitat.

Even though she has seen so much destruction of these animals she loves, and knows how cruel humans can be to animals and to each other, Jane Goodall has hope. She lists four reasons for that hope: we are starting to understand the threats to the earth and life on it, and surely we can deal with that; the human spirit is amazing and can accomplish what may seem impossible and inspire others to do the same; nature is amazing and can renew itself in seemingly impossible circumstances, bringing back plants and animals from the edge of extinction. Her final reason for hope is "the tremendous

"Change happens by listening and then starting a dialogue with the people who are doing something you don't believe is right."

—Jane Goodall

energy, enthusiasm and commitment of a growing number of young people around the world."

Let us go on, she says, "with great hope, for without it all we can do is eat and drink the last of our resources as we watch our planet slowly die. Let us develop respect for all living things. Let us try to replace impatience and intolerance with understanding and compassion. And love."

Dai Qing

1941 -

A Voice Against the Flood

Dai Qing (pronounced Dye Ching) was born to risk and danger. In fact, she was born bruised from the beatings her mother had suffered while being tortured as a spy during World War II. Her father was also imprisoned, tortured, and in 1943, when Dai was two, he was executed.

Dai's parents were loyal Communist Party members in China. When Japan attacked China in 1937, they became espionage agents in Beijing and spied on the invaders. They were caught and tortured. Dai Qing's mother suffered water torture and electric shock as well as beatings. She survived

and was released with her baby. Once out of prison, she got help from high Party officials, one of whom was a general in the People's Liberation Army. He adopted Dai after her birth-father's death, and because of his position, he was able to make sure she got a good education.

In 1966, Dai graduated as an electrical engineer. That same year she published her first article. She had married while she was at university and had given birth to a daughter. Because her daughter had no books to read, Dai wrote an article that asked why Chinese children had no books while children in other countries often did. That article about children's books was her first public questioning of a government that was not used to being challenged. This was also the start of her work as both an engineer and a writer.

Dai went on to study oil and missile engineering in Japan, then went to work for China's military intelligence as an engineer developing guided missiles. During this time she also studied English.

The Chinese Cultural Revolution began in 1966 and lasted for ten years. During that time China's leader, Mao Zedong, tried to change the basic structure of Chinese society. This was a very difficult time when many teachers, writers, and thinkers were killed, and millions more were sent to the country to live and work as "peasants." The conditions were harsh, many people were spying on each other, and discussion of almost any topic could be dangerous for individuals and their families.

Mao Zedong

Because they were highly educated, Dai Qing and her husband, like many intellectuals, were forced to go to a farm

run by the army in a remote area. For three-and-a-half years they raised pigs and worked the land in very harsh conditions, with only the most primitive tools. What was worse was that their baby daughter had been taken away from them to be raised by a working-class family. For Dai Qing, this marked the end of any respect or loyalty she felt for Mao's People's Liberation Army, which she now saw as nothing but an armed political organization.

When she and her husband were released, they returned to Beijing to find their daughter. Dai no longer had any desire to work as a government engineer. She had, however, been interested in journalism since she had written that first article in 1966. When she was offered a job at the Beijing *Enlightenment Daily*, she eagerly went to work for this newspaper that was read by thoughtful people.

Between the end of the Cultural Revolution in 1976 and the uprising in Tiananmen Square in 1989, people in China enjoyed a freedom of speech they had never before experienced. Dai was allowed to write pretty well whatever she wanted. She enjoyed writing fiction and published books of short stories. At the same time, she wrote the history she knew from her experience of the Communist Party. Most significantly, it was while she was working at the *Enlightenment Daily* that she became aware of an environmental disaster that was in the making in China: the Three Gorges Dam.

People have built dams for centuries. There are dams all over the world, including such famous ones as the Hoover Dam, on the Colorado River in the U.S., and the Aswan Dam, on the Nile River in Egypt. What makes the Three Gorges Dam different? Why might it be a disaster for China? How did Dai Qing become involved to the point where she has now spent more than twenty years as China's leading environmentalist, and the world's most public opponent of the dam?

In some ways, the Three Gorges Dam is no different from

dams in general. What most people don't know is that the huge modern dams constructed in the last eighty or ninety years are considered to be among the greatest ecological catastrophes that humankind has ever created. Dams change the river systems of the world in ways no one really understands, and will produce as-yet unknown consequences. Often, and this is certainly true of the Three Gorges Dam, in order to build a dam and contain the water it holds back, good farmland is flooded. Huge numbers of wild animals are killed in the flooding and millions of people are forced to move somewhere else. These people often lose not only their homes but also their only way of making a living. The possibility always exists that the dam may fail and cause tragic downriver flooding. Most mega-dams are built to generate electricity. But building a dam takes years and huge amounts of money. Once a dam is complete, several more years go by before the dam can create electricity and earn

The Yangtze River in China — on the left you can see the construction of the Three Gorges Dam

income. During this time, the tremendous financial strain can cause severe hardship for millions of people.

The lakes that dams create are often used as reservoirs for drinking water for large cities. But these lakes collect the soil that washes downstream — much of it good topsoil and rich sediment. When there is no dam, most of that soil continues on downstream. Portions of it collect beside the riverbanks and create rich new soil for farming along many miles of river. When there is a dam, however, the sediment collects behind the dam and gets into its machinery and moving parts, interfering with or destroying its ability to function. Dealing with the sediment is hugely expensive. Perhaps even worse, this sediment, originally so rich and productive for growing food, stagnates and breeds dangerous, even poisonous, algae, fungi, and insects. Fish die. Animals that drink the water or that rely on plants around the lake die. What had once been rich

The Three Gorges Dam site in Hubei, China

> "I am not optimistic. Some people, more and more people, have environmental sense, but most of the 1.2 billion people in China have no sense of nature and just want to get rich...human beings are going to destroy the environment."
>
> —Dai Qing

farmland is either submerged or poisoned by the water it relied on for life. Crops fail. People lose their incomes and their food supply. Eventually, people die. Egypt is experiencing all these things because of its Aswan dam. The soil beside the Nile River, which for thousands of years was some of the richest soil in the world, is now a dust desert. Thriving farms no longer exist. People who had been prosperous are poor; the people who were poor are desperate. Food is scarce and horrendously expensive.

The Yangtze River, known as the River of the Three Gorges, is the third-largest river in the world. The Three Gorges Dam will be the largest dam in the world. It will cost more than $24 billion, and the land it floods will be an area four times the size of California. More than a million people, farmers of rich soil that produced 60 percent of China's wheat, have been moved up the mountains to rocky barren places where farming is poor or impossible. The dam will flood a hundred thousand acres of farmland. It will forever bury thirteen towns, along with their 657 factories, deep under water. No one knows what toxic materials may leech from those factories into the drinking water of millions of people. The bedrock in that area is unstable, and no one knows how well or how long it will stand up to flooding. The dam will severely interfere with river navigation. The Yangtze River Valley is one of the world's richest locations for fossils from the Paleolithic era. Water will first bury, and then destroy, all this important historical evidence. And that valley is the most beautiful river valley in the world. That, too, will be gone — forever.

No one really knows what all the consequences of a project like the Three Gorges Dam will be. But there is every reason to expect that all the disasters known to occur because of dams will happen in China. If, or when, these predictions become true, the human, animal, plant, and environmental costs will be unimaginable.

While she was working at the *Enlightenment Daily*, Dai learned of the plans for the dam and of the environmental disasters that scientists and environmentalists predicted if the dam went ahead. In 1989, she gathered a group of essays that had been written by people aware of the dangers of the Three Gorges Dam, and she published them in her book *Yangtze! Yangtze!* The book received a lot of media attention and was widely read by both supporters and opponents of the project. This marked the first time opponents had been heard, and the first time any kind of debate on an environmental issue had been opened in China. Although the government voted to go ahead with the project, Dai considered the debate to be both an environmental and a human rights victory. In a society that did not tolerate debate, lively discussion was not only happening but also was building.

In July 1989, Dai Qing was arrested for voicing her opinions. She was sent to a prison where many people languish for years without ever being charged for any crime. Dai spent ten months there, six of those months in solitary confinement. She was not allowed to read, to write, or to see anyone but the occasional guard. She spent only half an hour each day outside her cell in a concrete passageway, where only one prisoner at a time was allowed. She never saw anyone else who was jailed there.

In 1950, there were two large dams in China. In 1985, there were 18,820, half of all the world's dams.

The government banned her book and destroyed all the copies they could find. Then, for some reason, perhaps because she is so well known and influential, she was released.

Since leaving prison, Dai has been under constant surveillance. She is often followed. Her phone is tapped. Despite this, she has managed to write and speak in China, and around the world. Her huge effort to get the dam either stopped or scaled down in order to decrease environmental danger and the damage to people, animals, and farmland continues. While international opposition to the project has grown and loans for its construction have been cancelled, other sources have come forward with money to build the dam.

Still, Dai speaks out. For example, she said in a lecture in Boston in 1996: “The Three Gorges project is the product of a decision made by a single party — the dictator...who has the notion of...being able to easily create something that is humongous...and that this is a reflection of his greatness.” And in late 2006, she called the dam project “a goldmine for corrupt officials.” *Yangtze! Yangtze!* has been translated into English and published in Canada and Britain, and Dai has written many articles and another twelve books. One of these, *The Red River Dragon has Come*, talks about the failure, in 1975, of a total of sixty-two dams in eastern China. This is the first time the rest of the world has heard about that catastrophe, in which somewhere between 86 and 230 thousand people died and another 12 million people suffered famine or disease. It is estimated that if the Three Gorges Dam fails, the resulting disaster will be forty times the size of the 1975 failure.

Dai’s work has been acknowledged far beyond her home country. She won a prestigious fellowship at Harvard University in 1991. The International Association of Poets, Playwrights, Editors, Essayists, and Novelists (PEN) is a highly respected and influential global organization that honors and works to protect writers who are in danger, and who stand up for human rights. Dai received the PEN International Award in 1992. That same year she won the Condé Nast Traveller Award. In 1993, she received the Goldman Environmental Prize, and in 1996, she gave the Freeman Lecture at the Massachusetts Institute of Technology (MIT). The more she speaks and becomes recognized and honored around the world, the more she is able to speak up in the one country where she will probably never be honored: her own.

In November, 2006, the Chinese government executed a twenty-year-old protester against the Three Gorges Dam. His lawyer and family found out about his death only after it had happened.

Dai Qing's success is that her work has focused world attention on the Three Gorges Dam. Sadly, the dam is now in the final stages of preparation to open. Dai Qing is not happy about this disaster in the making. Nor does she believe that her country will make any real environmental progress in the next decades. Most people are greedy, she believes. Because her people have been poor for generations, she sees them going after material wealth — at the cost of the environment. Still, supported by her mother, her husband, her daughter, and her six siblings, she continues her work, not because she is optimistic, but because she must.

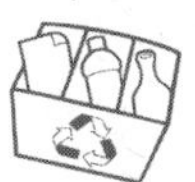

Fatima Jibrell

1948 -

Reclaiming a Ravaged Land

As a child, she was kept inside her family's hut so that she wouldn't wander into Somalia's tall waving plains of grasses, grasses that provided food for both people and animals — including lions. Since that time, Somalia has changed dramatically. So has Fatima Jibrell.

Fatima grew up in Somalia and then spent several years studying in the United States, where she married and had two daughters. During that time, conditions in Somalia grew worse and worse. By the end of the 1980s, political unrest was threatening to turn into war. Drought was killing thousands

of people, and millions more were in danger. While she was still in the U.S., Fatima started the Horn of Africa Relief and Development Organization. Now called Horn Relief, the organization started out raising money to provide emergency aid and supplies — such as food, blankets, and medicine.

In 1991, Fatima and her family returned to live in Somalia so that she could be in her country to help. A major part of that help was establishing Horn Relief in northern Somalia. That year, the government totally collapsed. Warlords were leading vicious battles, and the country was in full-scale civil war. Somalia still has no central government, and as this story is being written, new violence, which started in the southern part of the country, has spread to the north, where Fatima is.

The war, drought, starvation, and lack of health care drove millions of people out of their homes and into huge refugee camps. Three hundred thousand civilians died. Elderly people, children, and pregnant women were especially affected, as were the livestock that had fed the people. The lives of 4.5 million more people were threatened. Speaking of her return to Somalia, Fatima said, "The civil war in my country was so terrible and caused so much suffering that I wanted to do something for the internal refugees and victims."

As the war went on, the environmental destruction grew worse and worse. Vast areas of Somalia became desert, where little or nothing could grow. The grasslands Fatima had known as a child disappeared. Wild animals died. The livestock that had provided food and milk for the people also died. These animals had been Somalia's largest export to the neighboring countries, so the income from selling the animals also dwindled. Then the countries that had imported the animals banned them, destroying what was left of that income.

Somalia's biggest export then became charcoal. To make the charcoal, huge numbers of acacia trees, some as much as five hundred years old, were burned in enormous kilns. Clear-

cutting the trees destroyed the forests of Somalia, and smoke from the kilns polluted the air, making breathing difficult and destroying some plants. As the supply of trees dwindled, most of what was left of the grasses and other small vegetation that had once fed animals was ripped out to fuel the fires of the charcoal kilns.

Horn Relief had grown in the U.S., and it caught on and grew in Somalia and in Kenya, to the south. With Fatima's leadership, the organization went from providing emergency supplies to developing ways to help rebuild the country. It established ongoing medical clinics, schools, and literacy programs. People from Horn Relief also went out to the farmers and nomadic peoples to teach them to grow food and to breed and raise cattle in the desert conditions that had come into being in the country.

In the mid-1990s, Fatima joined with others to form two more badly needed organizations. When a new political crisis broke out in the Puntland region in northeastern Somalia, bringing with it the threat of even more death and starvation, Fatima and a group of other women started the Women's Coalition for Peace. The group works to keep peace in the region. It helps give women a voice in politics, a voice they have never had, even though, as Fatima points out, "Women are the backbone of the communities." She also helped form the Buran Rural Institute (BRI), which promotes peace, environmental health, and participation in political issues and organizations by people who do not usually work in politics.

> "Women are the backbone of the communities and the custodians of the environment. But they don't have the power."
>
> —Fatima Jibrell

During this time, too, Fatima became coordinator of the Resource Management Somali Network (RMSN), a group that helps people develop

the skills to do what they can with available resources. For example, little or no rain falls in Somalia. When the short rainy season does come, the earth is so dry and solidly packed, almost like bricks, that the rain just runs off and is lost. RMSN shows people how to build tiny, temporary dams out of rocks. People can use the water that collects behind these dams for drinking and irrigation. Unlike huge dams where the buildup of silt creates a problem, the soil these dams collect feeds new growth. People can actually grow food in a place that had been totally dry and barren. Eventually these plants take hold in the soil and help to keep the rain where it can be of most benefit. When enough plants grow together from one year to the next, the rock dams will be dismantled. This way, plant by plant, and if the bombing ever stops, Somalia can slowly become green once again.

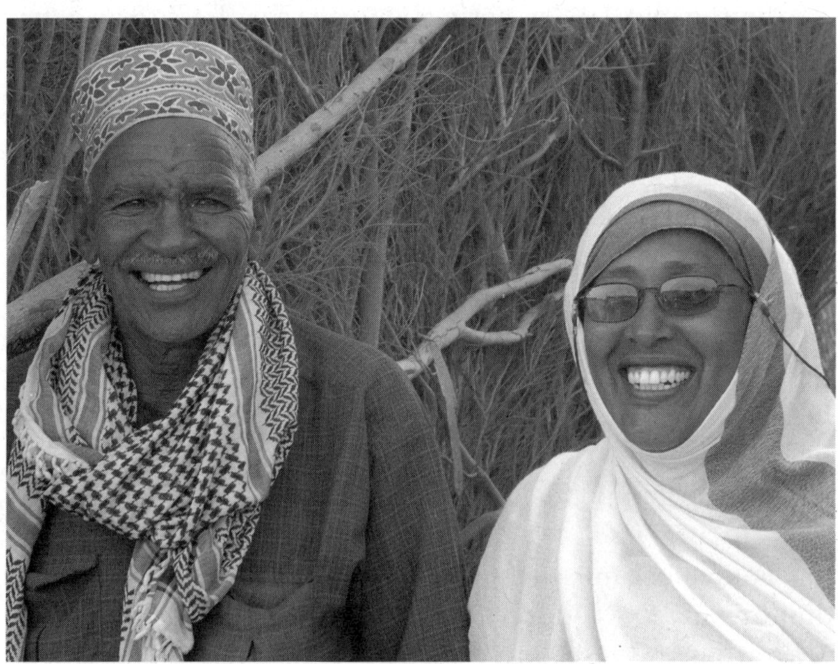

Fatima with her uncle in Duduri, Somalia. Fatima's early childhood was spent in this area

As Somalia's grasslands turned to deserts, seafood gained a new place in people's diet. This shift brought increased attention to the waters off Somalia's coast. In the late 1990s, Fatima, by now her country's leading environmentalist, included two more major issues in her campaigns: over-fishing by foreign ships and the illegal dumping of toxic waste off the country's coast.

Fatima's ongoing projects in the once lush, peaceful country that has turned into a war-torn desert now include several kinds of environmental issues. All of these concern people's basic right to eat. This means having clean water, being able to grow food on the land, and having access to healthy food from the sea. It also means saving what trees are left and working around the devastation caused by cutting and burning trees to make charcoal. Fatima recognizes that women are the backbone of society and that "90 percent of the work is done by women." Because women in Somalia traditionally have had no power, her environmental work includes both assisting women to participate in the public realm and working to make room for them in politics and government. And because war destroys life, health, and the very basis of society, she also works to end the vicious tribal fighting in her country.

The ongoing campaign to save trees and the environment from the effects of charcoal manufacturing is complex. Horn Relief and RNSM have been the only ones tracking the massive destruction of Somalia's forests. Charcoal is a traditional fuel for cooking in Somalia and exporting charcoal created many jobs. The questions became: If no one cares, and if there is no government to put a stop to exporting charcoal, what can anyone do? If people who create charcoal for export stop making it, they will lose their jobs. Then how will they live? And without charcoal and the grasslands that produced the other kinds of fuel, how can people cook their food?

Horn Relief has led the push to educate farmers, those who tend animals, and tradespeople. The educational programs help to provide jobs and to increase the ability to grow food in the new desert conditions in Somalia. Traditional nomadic life, when land is used only as long as it can easily support people and their animals, is perhaps the most respected way of living in Somalia. Fatima says that this way of life "is sustainable if it is respected and the grasslands and the water and the eco-system are respected." Hundreds of thousands of people have lived in camps and have only been able to stay alive by helping destroy the soil, plants, and animals that make life itself possible. Many of these people can now go back to living in a familiar, dignified way of life that feeds the land instead of further destroying it.

Horn Relief has also established schools for the children of workers in the charcoal industry. There, the children can develop practical skills their parents have not had so they will be better equipped to earn a living. The possibility of a better and healthier life for their children has provided added reason for people to stop making charcoal. As awareness grew, more and more people saw the damage charcoal-making was creating. By the time a central administration was set up for the northern and eastern parts of the country, enough people cared about the problem that the administration could ban almost all sale of charcoal abroad — and could enforce that ban. Horn Relief's campaign has been so successful that the business of manufacturing charcoal for export has almost entirely disappeared.

"Fatima's amazing. She's a bundle of energy. She works hard — she pushes and bullies. She's almost sixty and she hasn't slowed down at all."

—Jim Lindsay

But people have to cook. To replace charcoal as fuel, Fatima and Horn Relief imported several styles of solar cookers from Europe, the U.S., and other parts of Africa. But these cookers worked so slowly that people did not want to use them. A charcoal fire brings a litre of water to a boil in seven minutes; the goal was to find a cooker that would match that time. After many attempts with different sizes and shapes, a large, butterfly-shaped pair of metal cooking surfaces managed to cook as quickly as charcoal. In 2004, Fatima and Jim Lindsay

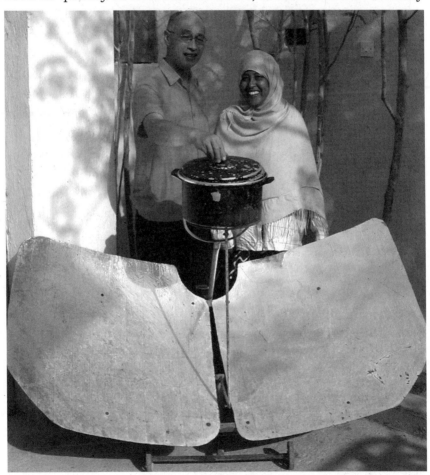

Fatima and Jim Lindsay demonstrate a Sun Fire Cooker

"Pastoralists follow rain and pasture in Somalia. They have goats, camels, sheep, and cattle, mostly…in Somalia it is probably the most respected lifestyle....And it is sustainable if it is respected and the grass lands and the water and the eco-system is respected. But…it is threatened."

—Fatima Jibrell

founded Sun Fire Cooking, which distributes cookers through Horn Relief and its related organizations. Jim is a former Australian diplomat who was already distributing solar cookers in China. Although the type of cooker used in China and now in Somalia is relatively cheap, buying one involves a lot of money for a Somali family or village. But when a village does purchase a cooker, the people who use it save enough money in one year from not buying charcoal to pay for it. The cookers are sturdy, they last twenty years, and they are very heavy, which is useful during Somalia's several months of high winds. The weight also helps prevent theft! Every half hour, the cooking plates are shifted by a simple mechanism to keep up with the movement of the sun. When placed in a village square, a number of people can use the cooker at the same time, and the only fuel needed is the sun. It will take many years for these cookers to make a major impact in Somalia, but the process has begun.

Fatima Jibrell's work has gained her international acclaim. She received the 2002 Goldman Environmental Prize, the world's largest grassroots prize for environmentalists. Her daughter, Degan Ali, has worked with her mother for several years and is vice-director of Horn Relief in Nairobi. She admires her mother and her "unbridled zest for work, her enthusiasm and optimism." That zest for work, enthusiasm, and optimism keeps Fatima Jibrell working, it seems tirelessly, in one of the most war-torn, famine-plagued, and environmentally robbed places on earth.

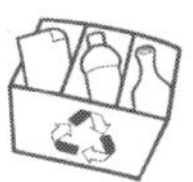      

Vandana Shiva

1952 -

Defending Earth Democracy

Vandana Shiva's work takes her from her mother's farm in India to the worlds of international politics, finance, and multinational corporations. It takes her from farmers, often women, who need seeds for their gardens so that they can feed their families, to scientific research laboratories. She moves from meetings with small grassroots organizations in remote areas to conferences of thousands of representatives of governments from all over the world.

Vandana grew up in Dehra Dun, in Uttaranchal State, in India's Himalayan foothills. Her father worked as a forester and

farmer, and her mother gave her children her love of the natural world. Once Vandana had finished school, that love — and her belief that it is possible to understand the natural world through science — took her to Canada. During her seven years away from home she completed a master's degree in physics at the University of Guelph and a doctorate in the philosophy of science at the University of Western Ontario. In 2002, Western also granted her an honorary doctor of laws degree.

Vandana was shocked when she returned to Dehra Dun in 1978. Vast areas of the ancient and much-loved forests that had provided food and work for the local people were gone, replaced by apple orchards imported from thousands of miles away. The way of life of the people was seriously threatened. While she had been studying, Vandana had discovered how easy it is for large companies and others in power to distort facts in order to justify massive destruction and increase their profits. She returned home to find exactly that happening in her own hometown.

Vandana joined the Chipko Movement, which had been started in the early 1970s to fight further destruction of the forests. "Chipko" is a Hindi word that means "to stick" (like glue). Since the members of the Chipko Movement stick to trees to save them, the word has come to mean "to save trees." Women run Chipko and do most of the work, almost all of it volunteer work. They are known as "India's tree huggers" because they have formed lines around trees and held onto them when necessary to prevent their being cut down These women have stood up to abusive company officials, beatings, chain saws, and guns. Despite the international forces against them, members of the Chipko Movement have saved vast areas of India's forests.

Vandana's first job when she returned home was as a research scientist with the Indian government. This work was only part of what she did, though. She spent ten years

researching how natural resources have been treated through history and particularly since the 1960s. At the same time her grassroots activism started to grow.

In the late 1970s, Vandana started Navdanya. This movement collects and saves the seeds of traditional, long-used plants in order to prevent species from becoming extinct. This is crucial work. When huge companies control a section of the global food supply, they use fewer and fewer varieties of plants. This practice both weakens the species and reduces people's ability to grow their own food.

Governments and corporations can influence the research they fund. Vandana, therefore, decided to set up her work so that it would never have to depend on money from outside sources. In 1981, she founded the Research Foundation for Science, Technology, and Natural Resource Policy, which researches the developing science and technology of agriculture. The Foundation now has offices in New Delhi. When she started it, though, Vandana had almost no money to go with her big plans, so she set it up in a place that charged very little rent — her mother's cowshed.

As a physicist, ecologist, and environmental activist, Vandana Shiva's work has been about agriculture, ecology, gender, and the power of politicians and multinational corporations. Her work has centered around issues that have come to be known as biodiversity, biopiracy (a term she introduced), and earth democracy. While it is possible to look at specific areas of her work, all parts of it are interconnected. It's possible to say that in a way these parts come together to form their own kind of ecosystem.

Biodiversity has to do with the varieties of living things that inhabit the earth. In any one area, as Vandana points out, species will have evolved so that they can survive in that soil and climate. There are millions of ecosystems across the planet, each with its own inhabitants, needs, and balances.

In 1992, Vandana Shiva was one organizers and one of the fifteen hundred women from eighty-three countries to attend the World Women's Congress for a Healthy Planet. The event gave her the most inspiration she had known in a decade. A few months later she attended the UN Earth Summit in Rio de Janeiro. There, she observed, "99 percent of the delegations just sit there without any commitment.... They are 99 percent men and 99 percent of them have orders not to do anything."

These ecosystems are very complex and consist of huge numbers of interactions among the plants, animals, insects, sea creatures, other living organisms, and the place they live in. These interactions help to keep the air, soil, and water — and those who rely on them — healthy. Evolution continues. Unless someone or something interferes with it, that evolution will go along as it needs to, and in a way the ecosystem can support. What one species produces or takes from the area, another species may very well put back. For example, humans and other animals breathe in oxygen and breathe out carbon dioxide. Carbon dioxide is poisonous to us, but plants need it. They breathe in large amounts of carbon dioxide, and breathe out oxygen. One sure way to disrupt the balance of an ecosystem is to remove too many types of plants, animals, birds, or elements of the soil from an area and to bring in too much of something else. In other words, mess with the system long enough and hard enough and it will break down. The soil or water will eventually die and so will everything in and around it.

While life has often been hard around the globe, people have never poisoned and destroyed soil, plants, animals, birds, fish, and themselves. Never, that is, until now. Biodiversity

is essential to life on the planet. Multinational companies are planting far too much of one thing in areas all over the world. They are stripping huge areas of their natural diversity, flooding the world's soil with chemicals, and replacing human energy with technology and fossil fuels. Vandana Shiva has stepped forward to become one of the world's foremost defenders of biodiversity.

Biopiracy has to do with the theft of the right to grow and use certain plants. That theft happens when a company in a rich nation takes out patents on a particular plant or on the seeds of that plant. A handful of companies have already done this and continue to patent all kinds of seeds. The plants involved are ones that for centuries have provided food and/or medicine, usually in poor countries. When a company patents a plant, it controls *all* use of that plant. The people who have traditionally used these plants must suddenly buy seeds. It becomes illegal to plant the seeds without paying for them, even if the plants have always grown wild in your garden. Basmati rice, a staple of the Indian diet, is one example. Another is the neem tree, which repels certain harmful insects without damaging other plants or animals. People who have used the neem tree for centuries must now either pay to use it or buy manufactured insecticides, some of which are known to have toxic side effects. People who cannot afford to buy insecticides lose valuable food and are exposed to the harmful insects. As well, some companies have genetically altered seeds so that they will not reproduce. People who have relied on these plants and collected their seeds year after year for centuries must now buy seeds every year — if they can afford to.

Not all, but many of these biopirated seeds come from what are known as southern countries, like India, not the richer northern countries. Efforts to make money in some parts of the world have created huge hardship, even starvation, in other parts. What makes this even worse is that the southern countries have often freely shared their plant resources with the northern ones. Then companies in these richer countries have "stolen" those resources. Like many people, Vandana believes that it is immoral and illegal to claim to "own" things that grow, and by doing that to take away people's ability to have food. Opposition to the buying and selling of "ownership" of life is another huge part of her work. This opposition often takes place at the local level. It has come to be known as earth democracy.

Earth democracy springs from a very ancient part of Indian thought that considers all inhabitants of the earth as family. "Indian cosmology," Vandana points out, "has never separated the human from the non-human — we are a continuum." This means that we are all part of the same larger whole. As she also points out, many other cultures, notably North American First Nations, share this kind of thinking. If we are all part of the "earth family," it is not possible to patent or own life. Vandana puts it this way: "Life is not an invention. Life cannot be a monopoly. You cannot sell us the seeds you stole from us, and you cannot charge us royalties for the product of nature's intelligence and centuries of human innovation."

The second part of earth democracy involves taking back the right to look after biodiversity and to use it in sustainable ways. This sounds like a simple and obviously reasonable way to live. But big companies believe they can destroy biodiversity and engage in biopiracy in order to make money. The right to live, to eat good food, and drink clean water has become a global battle of rich against poor. It is the struggle of earth-killers against people who wish

"Women have a distinctive perception of what life is, a sense of what is really vital, which colors their view of what is at stake in the world."

—Vandana Shiva

Vandana Shiva in 2007

to preserve the earth and its health, bounty, and beauty.

Vandana's work goes on in many places. She works with grass-roots organizations to take back people's right to live in a healthy way and to grow healthy food in healthy soil. She campaigns against the huge corporations that don't care about the soil or about tomorrow. She speaks all over the world to promote safe foods, not ones that have been genetically altered in ways that may harm those who eat them. She points out that using huge areas of land for a single crop, instead of for many different ones, is a disaster in the making. For a short time, this kind of farming creates wealth for a few people who live far away from the land in question. On that land, however, people get pushed out of their homes. They can no longer make a living, and the land becomes an exhausted desert in just a few years. And, she points out, no amount of money will save anyone if the planet and everything on it are doomed.

Campaigning for women's rights is central to Vandana's work. She realizes that women work hardest to provide food for the people around them. Women are most closely connected to life and they are the ones who most quickly notice and understand threats to life. Women are the poorest members of society, and women and their dependents suffer most from interference with the environment. Despite all these difficulties, women work hard for environmental causes of all kinds all over the world. Vandana

believes that women must have a public presence and public power so they can work effectively in this struggle.

In addition to setting up environmental and women's groups, meeting with organizations, and speaking at conferences, Vandana's hundreds of articles and many books about the fight to save the earth have been published all over the world. The titles of her books show her courage. They include: *Water Wars; Stolen Harvest: the Hijacking of the Global Food Supply;* and *Biopiracy: The Plunder of Nature and Knowledge.* As well, her work has been recognized with many prizes and awards. One of these, the Right Livelihood Award, is considered the alternative Nobel Prize.

"As a citizen of India, I've asked myself how a society that is the cradle of peace, the land of Gandhi and Buddha, could be reduced to one of the most volatile societies in the world."

—Vandana Shiva

The work Vandana has been doing for thirty years is huge, even overwhelming. When asked how she stays so full of personal, mental, and spiritual energy, she replied, "I do not allow myself to be overcome by hopelessness, no matter how tough the situation." She went on to say that she's learned not to look at the results of what she does, because she can't control that. What she can control is what she herself does, how she uses her passion and commitment. Doing what she can and not trying to control what she can't, allows her, she says, "always to take on the next challenge because I don't cripple myself, I don't tie myself in knots." She is also excited to be part of an approach to activism "that centers on the protection of life, celebrating life, enjoying life as both our highest duty and our most powerful form of resistance against a violent and brutal system." Obviously, Vandana's approach works. Her energy continues, and her incredible work keeps on growing.

Sheila Watt-Cloutier

1953 -

Leading the Cry Against Poisoning the North

POPs? A rock group? Someone's dad? A sugary cereal? Maybe. But in Sheila Watt-Cloutier's part of the world, POPs are poisoning babies before they are born. In her work with her Inuit community and with the Inuit Circumpolar Conference (ICC), Sheila has spent more than two decades as a leader in the fight for environmental health in the North and around the world. Persistent Organic Pollutants (POPs) are toxic chemicals that do not dissolve but stay in the soil and waters of the planet and then collect in the bodies of people and animals, making them sick, or even killing them. Because

POPs are most concentrated in the waters of the North, they are particularly deadly for the Inuit.

Sheila's journey to leadership has been long in some ways and short in others. In many ways her story is the story of her generation of Inuit. She was born in Kuujjuaq in northern Québec. Her single mother supported herself, her own mother, and Sheila and her siblings. Because their mother had to travel in her work, the children grew up with their grandmother. Sheila was born on the land, into a way of life that had changed little for centuries. Hers was the traditional world of the Inuit, a society of nomads who lived by hunting, fishing, and gathering food from the land. They traveled over the ice and snow by dogsled in winter and through the waters of the North by canoe in summer. Ptarmigan, goose, fish, caribou, seal, and whale, which Sheila's brothers caught and which are still her favorite foods, were staples of the family's diet. These ancient traditions formed the base of Sheila's life.

When she was ten, Sheila left home to go to school in Churchill, Manitoba, and then in Nova Scotia. After high school, she attended McGill University in Montréal, taking courses in counseling, human development, and education. In her early twenties she worked as an Inuktitut-English interpreter at the hospital in Ungava, on the east coast of Hudson Bay in Québec. While she was there, she developed a lifelong interest in better health care and in the condition of education in the North. After leaving Ungava Hospital, she participated in the government-sponsored 1991-95 review of the educational system in Northern Québec. She contributed to the acclaimed report that came out of that review, *Silatunirmut: The Path to*

"The Arctic is vulnerable and fragile. What is happening in the Arctic now will happen to others further south in years to come. We are all connected."
—Sheila Watt-Cloutier

Wisdom, and to a video for teenagers, *Capturing Spirit: The Inuit Journey*. Then, for the next four years, she oversaw the administration of the Makivik Corporation. Set up in 1975, the corporation manages the $120 million the Inuit received as compensation for lands they lost under the James Bay and Northern Québec Agreement. Makivik Corporation owns several companies. It invests in businesses like airlines and communications companies that relate to the needs of the Inuit. And it provides money for social service programs and employment to improve life for Inuit communities.

These impressive public accomplishments took place in a complex and dramatic setting. Within Sheila's lifetime, Inuit society has changed beyond all recognition. From independent, strong communities living off the land, the Inuit have gone — in one generation — to living in settled communities with interference from outside at every level of their lives. They have been forcibly moved and removed from their ancient lands. They have lost control over their own lives, including language, health care, education, and day-to-day activities. In the process, the Inuit lost much of their sense of community and well-being. They were dragged from a social system that worked for them into a strange, foreign, and unwanted way of living that poisons their minds, bodies, souls, and spirits.

The changes are so vast, difficult, and even hostile, that the Inuit of Canada have one of the highest suicide rates in the world. Alcoholism and drug use are rampant. And until very recently, hopelessness and despair among Canada's Inuit have seemed too huge and powerful to fight. Only in the last very few years have some members of Inuit society begun to take back control over their lives and social structure. This includes living off the land and being aware of the life the land can give and the lessons it has to teach.

Sheila Watt-Cloutier experienced this entire wave of change. She went from traveling only by dog sled and canoe to traveling all over the world by jumbo jet. She has gone from a world where people spoke only in their own language, Inuktitut, and only to their immediate community, to a multinational, multilingual Internet world. She has gone from being aware only of her family and close community to addressing huge international gatherings.

In the midst of all this upheaval, it was discovered in the mid-1980s that people of the North were taking in high levels of toxic substances. In some cases, these were the highest levels in the world. The Inuit live nowhere near the sources of these pollutants. They do not benefit from the uses of those chemicals. But they are being poisoned by them. Sheila studied the reports that showed that there were "more than two hundred chemicals, including DDT, PCBs, dioxin, lead, mercury, toluene, benzene, and xylene" in mothers' breast milk and in the umbilical cords of newborn babies. Inuit children were being born with poisons in their systems. "These were found in mothers' milk, not in some hazardous-waste site," she wrote. "We were being poisoned — not of our doing but from afar."

What makes things worse is that global warming, which is also caused by activities of societies far away, is melting the ice of the North. Where there had been solid ice masses, the arctic ice is turning to water, or thinning to become a water-and-ice soup that is impossible to travel across. Insects that had always been controlled by the cold and ice are invading many places, eating vegetation, and making humans and animals miserable. Animals and birds from the South are going into the far North: in 2005, for the first time, robins were seen in Inuvik. Polar bears are having trouble finding food, are growing thinner, and in some places they are drowning because they cannot swim the distances between solid places, and are unable to rest. Traditional food is becoming scarce and difficult to get. Airfields have become unstable, and houses are splitting apart as the ground beneath them shifts and crumbles. The very land that is the base of Inuit life is disappearing.

"Faced with this stark reality," says Sheila, "I brought a sense of responsibility and commitment, urgency and passion to my work." She goes on to say that although she was elected to the Inuit Circumpolar Conference to work on "global issues — including the protection of our environment — there can be no doubt that [this work] led my personal and professional journeys to mirror each other. As I work to help the world rid itself of its man-made toxins, a parallel process is happening in my own spirit, as deep-rooted legacies of generational wounds that have left their mark deep in my soul are now, through my own cleansing, leaving my body and spirit."

Sheila has needed all her sense of responsibility, commitment, urgency, and passion. The Inuit Circumpolar Conference represents the 155,000 Inuit of Canada, Greenland, the United States, and Russia. Although the term "Inuit" does not appear in the languages of the communities of Alaska and Russia (they refer to themselves as "Yupik"), ICC members have agreed to the name Inuit to refer to members from all four areas. The organization's goal is to promote unity among Inuit peoples, ensure that Inuit culture continues to develop and thrive, and to foster the rights and interests of Inuit people internationally. In 1995, Sheila was elected president of the Canadian Inuit Circumpolar Conference. Three years later she was re-elected, and in 2002 she began a four-year term as chair of the international ICC.

"Inuit have knowledge and wisdom to offer the world. We are committed to engaging governments, industry, business and commerce, and non-governmental organizations. All of us must learn to live sustainably in our global village."
—Sheila Watt-Cloutier

As chair of the Canadian and then the international ICC, Sheila had a demanding schedule, meeting with media of all kinds to raise the

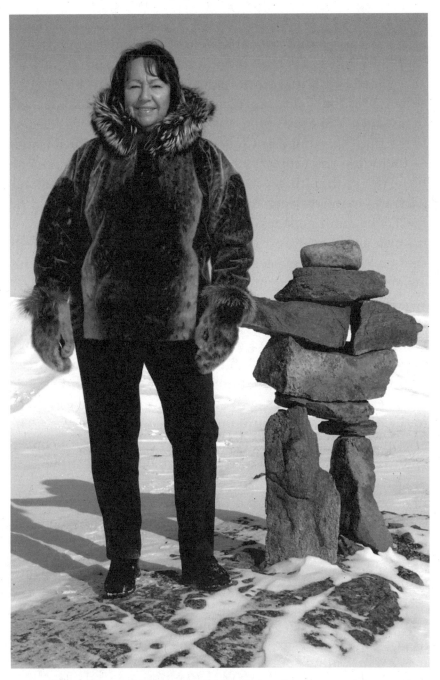

Sheila Watt-Cloutier with an inukshuk, a stone figure sometimes used to guide travelers in the Arctic

profile of Inuit people in the world outside the North. She did interviews, wrote articles, and was featured in several documentaries. But the main activities of her first years in office centered around convincing nations of the need for an agreement to eliminate POPs. She then went on to participate in the meetings that led to that agreement, which is known as the Stockholm Convention. As spokesperson for the world's Inuit, she worked with representatives of many countries to draft this legally binding agreement that outlaws the nine worst persistent organic pollutants, including DDT (except for its use in the prevention of malaria) and PCBs. The signing countries examine new potential pollutants as they appear on the market and ban those that do significant damage and take a long time to disappear from the world's water and food supplies. The long and difficult negotiations for the agreement took place over several years and were finally completed in 2001. The Stockholm Convention went into effect in May 2004, with 151 signing countries.

Since then, Sheila has turned her attention to global warming and its effect on the North and on the Inuit. As she points out, even while some people were still questioning whether global warming was real, the Inuit were daily seeing and experiencing its effects. She uses storytelling, an ancient practice among the Inuit, to illustrate her point. She emphasizes that the North is the "canary in the cage" for the planet. She is referring to the practice of miners who used to take a caged canary underground with them; if the canary died, the miners knew they had to get out before the poisonous gases that killed the bird killed them, too. Sheila points out that we ignore the changes and threats in the North at our own peril. "We're meant to be the beacon, so that the rest of the world can understand what it's doing to itself."

In December 2005, Sheila and sixty-two Inuit elders and hunters from communities across Canada and Alaska filed a

petition to the Inter-American Commission on Human Rights. They stated that the huge amounts of greenhouse gases put into the atmosphere by the United States have violated the human and environmental rights of the Inuit of this continent as they are guaranteed by the 1948 American Declaration of the Rights and Duties of Man [Humanity]. Early in 2007, their case was turned down. It will not be heard internationally.

Sheila Watt-Cloutier has received many awards, both personally and on behalf of the ICC, for her work on POPs, education, traditional ecological knowledge, and the impact of climate change. These include the Global Environment Award from the World Association of Non-Governmental Organizations, in Washington, DC; the Sophie Prize, awarded in Oslo, Norway; the Champion of the Earth Award, from the United Nations, which she received in Nairobi, Kenya; the Citation for Lifetime Achievement at the Canadian Environment Awards, in Vancouver; the International Environment Award, presented at Earth Day in Toronto; an honorary Doctor of Law degree from the University of Winnipeg; and the Order of Greenland, presented to her as she was leaving the office of chair of the ICC in December 2006.

Sheila has returned to Iqaluit, the capital of Nunavut, where she now lives. Her daughter, who is an Inuit folk-singer and throat singer, her son, and grandson are also there. She is now a member of the National Round Table on the Environment and the Economy (NRTEE), working for sustainable development throughout Canada. She is writing a book titled *The Right to be Cold*, and in February 2007, she was nominated for the Nobel Peace Prize.

In 2005, Sheila was awarded the Norwegian-based Sophie Prize ($100,000US). The award cited her work on climate change, especially "her efforts to bring human and human rights perspectives and the concerns of Inuit and all Arctic residents to this global issue."

Sharon Beder

1956 -

Exposing the Corporate Towers of Power

Sharon Beder is both an activist and a detective. She is a leader in Australia's work on basic environmental issues, especially water quality. She has published ten books and more than 150 articles and conference papers, and is a pioneer and an apparently fearless investigator.

Environmentalists know that our planet needs a healthy balance of air, water, soil, plants, animals, fish, and birds. One part of Sharon's work relates directly to practical, grassroots work in those issues. She also investigates those who have the power to make decisions that have huge environmental impacts

In primary school, Sharon progressed through all the levels of gymnastics. In high school she took up fencing and cricket and won the girl's school regional championship in fencing.

around the world. She reveals the public relations tactics and smoke screens corporations use to give the impression that they are taking positive action, when in fact they are doing nothing — or worse. And she probes deep into government policies, and questions how governments make those policies. In doing this, she exposes what businesses and governments are really doing about environmental issues, as well as how they can mislead the public.

Sharon was the oldest of three sisters and grew up in Lower Hutt, a suburb of Wellington, New Zealand's capital city. Her mother was an office manager and her father first had a business trading wool, skins, and tallow (animal fat), then became an accountant. Most of the time the family lived comfortably.

When she was very young, Sharon went to gymnastics classes. In high school, she took up cricket and fencing, winning the regional girl's school fencing championship in her last year. Also in her final year of high school, she was elected head prefect. Head prefect — the head of the entire student body, including both girls and boys — was usually a boy, but in Sharon's year, she filled the position.

Sharon did well at school and enjoyed mathematics as well as drawing and painting. But because the school didn't allow her to do both in the upper grades, she had to choose one. She picked mathematics, and for a while thought she would like to be an architect. As time went on, though, she began to think that an architect could easily get bogged down in designing people's kitchens and bathrooms. When her father suggested that engineering might be more challenging, she decided he was right.

Though she didn't seem to realize it at the time, this is where Sharon's interest in the environment first appeared. The idea of designing bridges and large structures appealed to her. She then decided that she would like to use her engineering expertise to solve major world problems; perhaps she could use technology to provide food for starving people or develop environmentally sound energy sources.

The civil engineering class at the University of Canterbury had about one hundred students. Sharon and a girl from Malaysia were the only two women. Halfway through the course, Sharon started having second thoughts. She considered changing to agricultural engineering so that she could find ways to water the deserts and solve food problems. However, that would have meant changing universities or doing an extra year, and because she wasn't sure that agricultural engineering was the answer, she stayed at Canterbury and finished her degree in civil engineering. She graduated with first class honors in 1978.

Sharon went to work with the Ministry of Works in Wellington. After several months spent sitting in front of computers in the basement of a government building, she asked to be moved to a job that involved daylight and people. She was transferred to a position developing project management systems (systems to keep projects on schedule and on budget), and training engineers to use them.

After a year with the ministry, Sharon moved to Sydney, Australia. Her plan was that Sydney would be her first stop on a trip around the world. She got a freelance job as an engineer, at first designing bus-washing structures. That year she also met her

In engineering school, "I got on pretty well with the boys although they were very much into drinking and rugby, which I wasn't."
—Sharon Beder

future husband, and visited the United States. Back in Sydney, she worked for a company designing fire protection systems, including sprinklers. The rest of her world travels would have to wait.

In 1981, she tried to get an engineering job on a work site. "Apparently," says Sharon, "it was okay to have women working as engineers in the office, but on site was a different matter." She was given various excuses, including that "there were no toilets for women on site," and that "construction workers were a rough lot who swore a lot." At that time, she goes on, "engineering jobs were advertised in the 'Men and Boys' section of the *Sydney Morning Herald* classified job advertisements. One employer told me outright that he wouldn't employ a woman so I went to the anti-discrimination board, which investigated. They decided I should sue him, and put me in touch with a legal aid lawyer. However, the employer claimed that the small number of employees he had exempted him from the legislation. By this time I had another job — scheduling the work program for major engineering projects — so I dropped the whole thing."

In 1983, Sharon enrolled in a master's degree program in industrial engineering at the University of New South Wales ("I can't remember what the attraction was," she said). After one session of part-time study, she saw an advertisement for a master's program in science and society. This appealed more to her because it promised to explore the relationships among science, technology, and society. She completed the degree, and enjoyed it so much that she decided to do a PhD in the same area.

In her first PhD year, her husband became involved in campaigning against sewage pollution on Sydney's beaches. Sharon was so interested in the issue that she decided to write her thesis on the development of Sydney's sewerage system and the engineering decision-making involved. She was par-

ticularly interested in the political and social influences on that decision-making. It was this research, more than anything else, that got her active in environmental issues. She looked at the politics surrounding these issues and how companies used public relations to avoid environmentally sound decisions and actions.

She began to investigate how governments and corporations manipulate and mislead the public. These national and multinational powers give the impression that they are making good environmental decisions. But really, they may be doing nothing to prevent damage to the environment; sometimes they are actually increasing the damage in order to make more and more money.

Sharon has repeatedly pointed out the ways they do this. One way is to promise money for new action or a new approach to some issue without actually changing the way decisions are made. By doing this, the government or corporation can provide money for a project, but it makes sure that the project will not happen. For example, a corporation might allot money to buy trees to plant in an area where the company has clear-cut all the old growth. It may even put out a lot of money to buy seedlings. The company makes sure that the news media know about this. The news makes the company look good, as if it's acting in good faith. But the company does not make any money available to move the seedlings to the area where they are to be planted. Nor does it provide money to pay people to plant them. So the company looks good, but no trees have been planted. Another tactic is to keep discussions and decisions secret while pretending that they are public. The government or company holds public meetings, but ignores the ideas and suggestions that come out of those meetings. Sharon has exposed all these kinds of non-actions that are merely dressed up to look like actions. She has publicized secret studies made by industries. She has

revealed what companies and governments do, and how they do it. Her work has made her many grateful friends — and some powerful enemies.

While she was involved in these investigations, the computer was becoming part of daily life. It was believed that computers would save time and resources, notably paper, and would give people more time for leisure, friends, family, and healthy outdoor activities. Quite the opposite has happened: people are required to work more and more hours on the job, and then to work at home. People are expected to put their jobs before everything else in their lives and to be available via e-mail, cell phone, BlackBerry®, or other portable devices. Many people have come to believe that work is the highest good, above family, friends, recreation, contact with nature, a spiritual life, and even above their own health. Corporations tell their employees that working in their home office is a privilege. In fact, having employees work at home decreases the space those companies need to do business, and shifts the cost of things like heat, electricity, phones, and office equipment and supplies to home workers. People who work at home increase company profits. And paper and other resources are not being saved; their use has mushroomed. Sharon is one of the few people who have investigated and written about this process as an issue of the human environment.

While she was doing this environmental detective work, Sharon also worked as a part-time tutor and lecturer on environmental subjects. After she completed her doctorate in 1989, she turned her thesis into her first book, *Toxic Fish and Sewer Surfing: How deceit and*

The influence of Sharon's book on cleaning up the beaches of Australia, *Toxic Fish and Sewer Surfing: How deceit and collusion are destroying our great beaches,* won her a media prize from an unexpected source: the Australian Surfers Hall of Fame.

collusion are destroying our great beaches.

> "I liked the idea of designing bridges and large structures, and as I grew older and more idealistic I had visions of using my engineering expertise to find technological solutions to major world problems like providing food for the starving and environmentally sound energy sources."
>
> —Sharon Beder

During this time, too, she campaigned on the issue of beach pollution, and worked with Stop the Ocean Pollution (STOP). The group's efforts are a clear example of how a few people can make a big difference. STOP basically consisted of four people: Sharon, her husband, and two others. STOP participated in organizing a major concert that attracted 250,000 protesters against beach pollution. Their campaigns, combined with Sharon's research, led the *Sydney Morning Herald* to publish a major newspaper exposé based on her work. This exposé, about the destruction to life and health caused by toxic waste, ran for most of the year and attracted international coverage, including in *Time* and *New Scientist* magazines.

In the end, the government hired "independent" consultants who confirmed STOP's allegations about the pollution. The state government was forced to promise to implement a plan costing more than $6 billion over twenty years to upgrade the sewage treatment and take other measures to clean up the city's waterways. As Sharon's work so clearly points out, the promise of even huge amounts of money does not necessarily mean that anything useful will be accomplished But thanks to STOP's work, the people of Sydney are committed to this plan, and the work is progressing.

Sharon taught at the University of New South Wales for a year after she earned her PhD, then took a job at the University of Sydney, as the coordinator of environmental studies. In 1992, she moved to a lecturing position at the University of

Wollongong, near Sydney. She stayed there for fourteen years, teaching courses concerning science, society, and the environment. She was, as she puts it, "breeding a new generation of environmentalists." During that time she was promoted to full professor, wrote several books, and was involved in further environmental campaigns on various issues: a proposed national high-temperature incinerator; putting the site for the Sydney Olympics on top of a toxic waste dump; and treating timber with arsenic.

Sharon Beder has received national and international recognition for her research and writing. Journalists, scientists, and environmentalists have honored her as a leader. In 1990, she received a media prize from the Australian Surfers Hall of Fame because of her book and published research. In 1990, and again in 1991, she was nominated for the Eureka Prize for Environmental Research, and in 1992, received a prize for Excellence in Science, Technology and Engineering Journalism. She was awarded the World Technology Award for Ethics in 2001, and in 2003, was named one of Australia's top ten environmental thinkers. Engineers Australia named her one of "Australia's most influential engineers" in 2004.

Sharon now spends most of her time writing books. Three were published in 2006 alone: *Free Market Missionaries: The Corporate Manipulation of Community Values*; *Environmental Principles and Policies*; and *Suiting Themselves: How Corporations Drive the Global Agenda*. Like her earlier books, they expose the motives and actions of corporations and governments, and that provides ammunition for environmentalists in their struggle to restore the earth to health.

1958 -

Dedicated to the Amazon

Marina Silva grew up in the Amazon Rainforest of Brazil in an indigenous community where basic education and health care were impossible dreams. Her parents had eleven children, three of whom died. Marina, the oldest surviving child, helped care for her younger sisters and brother from an early age. While still very young she also joined her father and went to work as a rubber tapper.

In methods similar to tapping maple trees for sap, rubber tappers collect sap, which is natural latex, from rubber trees. A hole is bored into the tree and some of the sap drips

into a bucket. The tappers then collect the sap and sell it to rubber manufacturers. This method does not destroy the tree, but allows it to stay alive and healthy. Like the other rubber tappers, Marina walked almost nine miles (14 km) a day to do her work.

From her life and work in the rainforest, Marina learned the value of the forest for food, water, climate control, habitat, and employment. And she came to appreciate the value of resources that keep on producing. For example, keeping the rubber trees healthy instead of cutting them down maintains a valuable resource. Destroying the trees not only means the loss of a valuable resource, it changes the landscape in ways that destroy animal life, create drought where there had been water, and poison rivers that had been clean.

When Marina was fifteen, her mother died and all the care of the family fell to Marina and her father. Her mother had always managed the business end of the family's life, including calculating how much sap her husband and daughter had gathered and how much they needed to be paid for it. Since Marina's father could not do these calculations, she taught herself enough math to take on the task.

A year later, Marina became sick with hepatitis and was unable to do heavy work. Strange as it seems, this illness opened the world to her. Since she couldn't work, she asked her father to allow her to go to the city and do something that had only been a dream: attend school. Her father agreed. He encouraged her, in spite of the fact that it meant losing her help at home and the income she made from tapping rubber trees. Even though she was sick and alone, she went to the city, recovered from the hepatitis,

Marina was one of eleven children. Three died young, and she was the oldest surviving child, "So from a young age I helped to look after my six sisters and one brother."

then worked at her studies. In just three years she was able to pass all the entrance exams for university. In 1985, the child who had never set foot in a school until she was sixteen, earned a bachelor's degree in history.

When Marina's mother died, "I had to acquire some knowledge to help my father. Simple mathematics at first, in order to calculate the weight of rubber."

By that time, multinational corporations were clear-cutting or burning huge sections of the Brazilian rainforest. Mines there had to meet virtually no health or production standards, and were dumping all kinds of poisons into the rivers. When Marina returned home to the forest, the rubber tappers had formed a union. Their goals were to get better wages and working conditions and to gain some control over the land they worked on. This control would mean that their indigenous culture would stand a better chance of survival. It also meant that the workers could give better care to the trees they tapped. The outsiders who ran the operations neither lived on the land nor cared about it. But this rainforest was the workers' home; they needed and valued the land.

Marina went to work for the rubber tappers' union and its president, Chico Mendes. The two worked together both locally and more broadly in the trade union movement. Together, Marina and Chico founded the Workers Party, a political movement that still works for the rights of indigenous peoples and the welfare of their rainforest habitat.

By this time Marina had become an advocate of nonviolent approaches to political and social actions. She now put that approach to work. The tree tappers, their families, and supporters formed a human barrier campaign to oppose cutting down huge numbers of ancient trees. In a way that has since been used around the world, they put their bodies and

their lives between the trees and the companies that wanted to cut them down. This campaign saved millions of hectares of the trees that are the basis of the habitat of untold species of plants, animals, and indigenous Brazilians. The Amazon rainforest produces the most oxygen of any place on earth, so saving those trees and preserving that area benefits every living thing on the planet. Marina's work with union members and the Workers Party also won the right for traditional communities to manage these reserves. This action brought together two main themes of Marina's work: nonviolence and sustainable development. Sustainable development encourages an economy that does not damage ecosystems or people's wellbeing. It works for a better life for all people now, while making sure that people in the future can also have a good life.

Large, usually foreign, companies almost always believe that sustainable development interferes with their ability to make money. Those companies, along with other very powerful people, fight the trade unionists in Brazil. When Chico Mendes was assassinated in 1988, many people would have retreated from public action. Marina kept going. The press in Brazil began to call her an "Amazonian legend." They called her "a force to be reckoned with in the battle for the life and soul of the Amazon — the slash-and-burn developers and big landowners versus those who need the forest for their survival." In a country where trade union people and environmentalists have been terrorized and killed, she was standing up and being seen and heard. She was using nonviolent actions to oppose the most powerful forces in her country. She stood up against multinational corporations that had power in

Marina had a huge respect for Chico Mendes. "He knew how to listen and let everyone else speak, and only then would he make up his own mind. This is a very important lesson he left me."

Brazil and far beyond it. Her coworker and close friend had been murdered. Instead of backing down, Marina ran for city council in Rio Branco, the capital city of Acre, the state where she had been born. At the age of thirty, she received the largest number of votes ever cast for a city councilor.

Two years later, she ran for state deputy (the equivalent of state legislator or provincial member of parliament) and again received a huge number of votes. She now focused on the environment, including the rainforest, and indigenous rights, women's rights, and the rights of all people whom society usually tries to ignore. She was well aware, and so were her supporters, that these issues cannot be separated from one another. A healthy environment means healthy people, and people who are healthy, active, and involved can create and protect a healthy environment. This means all people, not just the few who have had power for centuries. Otherwise, big business could continue to destroy the environment.

After four years as a state deputy, Marina was elected to the Brazilian Senate. She was the youngest senator in the history of the country. The large daily newspaper in Acre, the *Jornal do Brazil*, called her win the "victory of the dream over circumstance." Again she won by a huge number of votes. In 2002, she ran again for the Senate and once again she won.

Marina Silva is frequently ill because of the effects of heavy metal poisoning, which she got from drinking water contaminated by mining and logging. Even though she spends long periods of time in hospital, after her re-election to the Senate she accepted an appointment to be Minister of the Environment. As cabinet minister, she is

"They say I am a fighter. I agree, but I think that, in myself, the fight comes after the dream."
—Marina Silva

in a position to continue to fight for the environment and for the people of the rainforest.

In May 2006, she chaired the Eighth Conference of the Parties to the Convention on Biodiversity (COP 8), which took place in Curitiba, Brazil. The conference was sponsored by the International Institute of Sustainable Development, whose headquarters are in Winnipeg, Manitoba, Canada, and which has thirty member nations. Environmentalists from all over the world attended the twelve-day conference. Their work focused on sea and coastal life, its protection, and the financial needs for continuing that protection. Fish and ocean life have become more important for Brazil than they used to be, since the country is growing more dependent on food from the sea.

Marina Silva with the Goldman Environmental Price in 1996

> "I have great admiration for people who struggle in the way Gandhi did: at once activist and pacifist."
> —Marina Silva

In an interview in November 2006, Marina talked with passion about the huge range of life in Brazil. Twenty percent, one in five, of the world's species of plants and animals live in her country. As long as logging, burning of forests, mining, and the theft of rights to seeds continue, those species are in danger. And as long as huge companies care only about taking as much money as possible out of an area, lush forests full of life will continue to turn into hostile deserts.

Marina Silva's health is not good. She is the mother of four children. And for more than twenty years she has responded to the needs of the indigenous peoples and the rest of the population of Brazil. Her work has taken her from small local communities and grassroots organizations to a huge role in government and the international environmental movement. She is also now a permanent member of the Brazilian Commission on Education and Social Affairs and the Amazon Development Policy Commission. She has earned international attention and has received many awards, including the Goldman Environmental Prize in 1996 and *Ms. Magazine*'s 1998 Woman of the Year Award.

Severn Cullis-Suzuki

1979 -

From Lemonade Stand to Global Stage

"I have no hidden agenda. I have come to fight for my future."

These are the words of a then thirteen-year-old Severn Cullis-Suzuki. She was speaking to thousands of delegates to the 1992 United Nations Global Summit on the Environment in Rio de Janeiro, Brazil. She spoke of starving children and animals, pollution, and global warming. She talked about the danger our planet is in, and the mess kids her age will inherit from the people who are now adults. Her speech stunned the delegates and brought world leaders to their feet with tears in their eyes.

How did she get there, and what does a person do after an experience like that?

Severn was born into a family of environmentalists. From the time she was very young, her parents and grandparents shared with her their love and knowledge of nature and of our planet. Her home was right at the water in Vancouver, so it was easy for her to learn about the plants and wildlife that either lived on the shore or washed up there. That's where her fascination with the environment began.

Her parents, she says, "are my best friends. They're amazing." Her father, David Suzuki, is a renowned scientist and environmentalist. Her mother, Tara Cullis, founded and runs the Suzuki Foundation. Severn admires her mother tremendously: "She works and works. She has so much energy and so much influence. The Suzuki Foundation was her idea. She works in the background and is invisible. That's always the way with women: they're invisible."

Severn's parents have made many things possible for her: "I've traveled and had education and opportunity. All these are amazing. But, my parents have always, from the time I was very young, listened to me. They respect me and listen to me. That respect and listening and taking me seriously from the time I was very little, that's the biggest gift. That's *the* gift."

Severn's first project had to do with saving the trees in the Stein Valley in British Columbia. Lumber companies had obtained permission to clear cut the timber in the valley. If the plan went ahead, it would destroy the ancient forests and an area that is sacred to First Nations peoples. It would also disrupt he fine-tuned balance of nature that supports a huge variety of plants and animals. Many organizations of First Nations and other people were working to prevent the destruction of this special place. Severn decided she needed to help. She sold lemonade and books in front of her house and sent the money she raised to supporters of the Stein Valley.

She was six years old and in kindergarten.

In 1989, Severn's father spent three months living with the Kyopo people in the Amazon rain forest of Brazil. These people live from the land, finding their food and medicine in the forest and the river. For clothes, they paint their skin. They live in mud huts, and they sleep in hammocks. Once his work there was finished, her father took Severn and her mother and sister to live with the Kayopo. They ate, swam, and gathered food together, and the visitors watched the Kayopo dance and sing. The visit and the people made a tremendous impression on Severn. As the plane rose to take her home, she could see the forest home of the Kayopo and the way logging was eating up the forest. She also saw the toxic waste from mines flowing into the rivers and the dense, black, choking smoke poisoning the air. This destruction was working its way toward her friends. It made her sad and angry. She decided that she had to do something to help.

"I spend a lot of time with First Nations people. Their influence has taught me a lot about our connection to earth and appreciation for the life forces that provide everything for us."

—Severn Cullis-Suzuki

Back in Canada, Severn told her school friends about her Kayopo friends and the way their world was being destroyed. She and a group of her Canadian friends started the Environmental Children's Organization (ECO). As she later told her listeners in Brazil, the ECO message is clear: "Children are the future, and the mess adults leave will be our home one day."

Severn is very good at gathering together groups of people who can accomplish far more than individuals can on their own. In order to be able to expand their work and spread their message, she and ECO connected with two more groups. One was the Environmental Youth Alliance (EYA), an established network of high school environmentalists. The other, Vancouver City Savings (VanCity), is a local credit union, which is known for its involvement with social justice issues. With the help of the high school students and money from the credit union, ECO put out three newspapers and sent them to elementary schools in Vancouver.

They also sponsored a speaker from Malaysia, who told how people there are being squeezed out of their homes in a way similar to how the Kayopo are being squeezed from theirs. In Malaysia, the water is so polluted that people can't drink, cook, or bathe with it. After the talk, ECO held bake sales and sold jewelry until they raised enough money to buy a water filter to send to Malaysia.

By this time, ECO and EYA had connected with groups of young environmentalists in many parts of the world. In 1991, Severn heard about the upcoming United Nations Conference on the Environment and Development (UNCED). This huge, twelve-day gathering in Rio de Janeiro brought together environmentalists and politicians from all over the world. The conference was really three conferences that overlapped. The Earth Summit was the official gathering of delegates and political representatives from many countries. A second conference, the Global Forum, included non-governmental organizations (NGOs) and other groups who do international work but are not connected to governments. The third, unofficial, conference brought together people who had not been invited to the other conferences. This type of gathering often includes the people who are most closely connected to the issues being discussed. These people also have the hardest time being heard — aboriginal groups, women, elders, and children.

The conference would take place in June 1992. First, ECO had to apply for a place in the Global Forum. That would mean that they would be allotted one of the six hundred booths there. With a lot of help from Severn's mom, the group put in their application — and it was accepted. Four members of ECO, Severn's sister and parents, and two other adults would go.

"I appreciate our [Canadian] health, wealth, and our air and water. Maybe one of our most important spiritual tasks in the West is to appreciate what we have."

—Severn Cullis-Suzuki

Sending that many people from Vancouver, British Columbia to Rio de Janeiro, Brazil would take a lot of money. Severn had sold lemonade and books to support the Stein Valley. She had sold jewelry and cupcakes to buy a water filter to send to Malaysia, and she had worked with VanCity to raise the money to publish newspapers. Now she and her friends would raise the even larger amount of money needed to take them to Brazil.

Once again they held bake sales. They made Fimo jewelry, including hundreds of ECO Gecko brooches. They organized a fundraiser with speeches and slides illustrating their activities to tell the audience why they needed to go to Brazil and what they would do there. They held an evening event at the Vancouver Planetarium and raised $4,700 in that one night. More donations followed, and before long they had the $26,000 they needed for the trip.

Brazil was an amazing experience. The Canadians saw unimaginable poverty and pollution. Beaches that had once been some of the most beautiful in the world were filthy and stinking. Children were living in cardboard boxes on the streets. What Severn and her friends saw made them question their life in North America. How could so many people have far more than they need, how could they waste so much, while in other places people starve?

The group set up the ECO booth at the Global Forum, including information, posters, and photographs showing

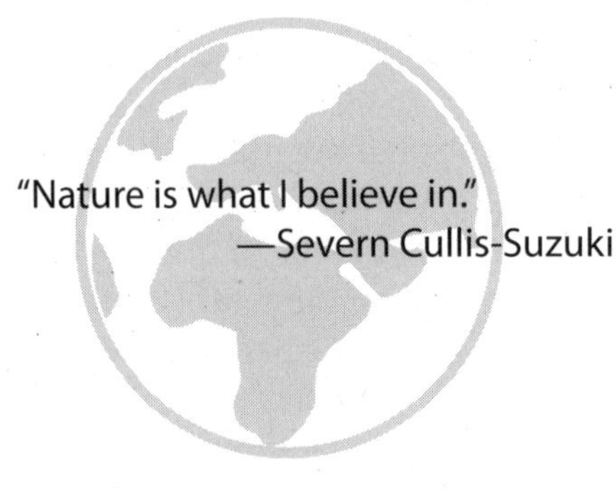
"Nature is what I believe in."
—Severn Cullis-Suzuki

their work. At least two ECO people were at the booth day and night to talk with the people who came by. The girls all spoke English and French, and Severn speaks a bit of Portuguese, the language of Brazil. They talked with politicians and especially tried to influence them. Severn's dad was speaking at several of the events at the conference. Each time he spoke he talked about ECO and invited its delegates to speak for a few minutes. They spent four days with a television crew from the Canadian Broadcasting Corporation, who put together a news story about ECO.

When Severn gave the speech for ECO, introducing herself as the spokesperson for a group of twelve- and thirteen-year-olds, she said that she was there to fight for her future. She spoke about animals who have nowhere to go because their habitat has been destroyed by pollution and global warming. She talked about the wealth of some parts of the world and the poverty of other parts. She noted that she has so much, while other children her age are scrambling to get food to stay alive, and she pointed out that the difference between her and those other children is simply the place they happened to be born. She emphasized that adults and their greed are destroying our planet and at the same time are deciding what kind of world children will inherit from them. She told the delegates that to say that everything will be all right isn't true and isn't good enough. Then she asked, "Are we [children] even on your list of priorities?"

The delegates were stunned. They hadn't expected to hear children speaking about the world adults are creating and that

children will inherit. Severn's speech was strong and blunt. And, perhaps most important, it was delivered by a child on behalf of children. Her words made a huge impression. She got a standing ovation and people had tears in their eyes. Together, Severn and her friends and supporters had delivered a tremendously important message. Many influential people and organizations, including the leaders of UNICEF, UNCED, and future U.S. Vice-President Al Gore, took her words to heart. There was huge news coverage, and the official United Nations film of the conference ended with clips from her speech. Severn and ECO's message was delivered around the world.

From that experience Severn learned several things. Individuals can accomplish a lot; a group of people can accomplish even more than a single individual. When that group is an organization of children, people will listen because they are so surprised to hear children speaking for themselves. It is easier for people in rich countries to make changes when they hear their children's worry, even fear, about how things like waste, toxic materials in our air and water, and global warming will affect their future. Parents hear their children's questions about whether there will *be* a future. And finally, she learned that children *can* do important things and make changes in our world.

Severn went to many more big conferences. She continued her studies, and shared her passion for our planet and the life on it with audiences around the world. And she watched for the impact of the UN Summit to emerge in world environmental projects.

That impact never came. "I thought speaking to world leaders would make a difference," she said. "It's been fourteen years since Rio. The 90s were a terrible decade for the environment. I came to realize that real change doesn't happen from the top. Politicians respond to what comes to them, they don't start things. It's individuals who can make a difference.

Severn spends much of her time speaking on environmental issues. In 1996, for example, she spoke at the University of Alberta (right) and in 2006 at the Green Toronto Awards

North Americans use ten times the resources that people in China do. That gives us a lot of power, each and every one of us. We need a groundswell, a big shift in understanding, and it's happening. Write, phone, or e-mail your government representatives. And at the same time, don't buy things in huge amounts of plastic packaging. Recycle. Reuse. Consume less. We've heard it all. And it works. Drive a more fuel-efficient car. Ride a bike. Walk. The shift is happening."

Severn's focus now is education, conservation, and traditional knowledge. She has visited many cultures in Canada, Southeast Asia, and South America, and has been adopted by three First Nations in Canada. She has seen what ancient traditions have to offer. She continues to speak at schools, conferences, corporations, and international meetings, including the UN Environmental Program's Global 500 Conference in Beijing. Her talks emphasize personal responsibility and the need to act with the future in mind. She stresses that young people can speak out and accomplish things to make a better future. She hosted "Suzuki's Nature Quest," a children's series broadcast around the world on Discovery Channel, and she has appeared on many other programs and given numerous interviews. She took part in a program to reduce, reuse, and recycle at home, and her family cut their garbage to almost nothing. Severn doesn't just talk about action on many levels, she takes action from her own kitchen to international, even global stages and TV programs.

In the summer of 2000, Severn and five girlfriends bicycled across Canada in the Powershift 2000 campaign for clean air. The next year, as part of her work at Yale University, she did research in a remote station in the Xingu Valley of the Brazilian Amazon. In the spring of 2002 she and her friends started the Skyfish Project, an Internet think-tank for which she writes regular articles as she travels. She spoke at the World Summit on Sustainable Development in Johannesburg,

South Africa in January 2003, and she is a member of the Special Advisory Board set up by Kofi Anan, who retired as head of the United Nations at the end of 2006.

Severn graduated from Yale University in 2002 with a science degree in ecology and evolutionary biology. She is now studying eelgrass for her master's degree at the University of Victoria in British Columbia. Eelgrass, the "grassy meadows of the sea," grows in all the world's oceans, and the young of 80 percent of marine species spend time in the safety and feed on the nourishment it provides. But all over the world eelgrass is declining. As one of many scientists investigating ways to preserve these nurseries for the ocean's young, Severn works with west coast First Nations people to rediscover how they traditionally used and managed eelgrass.

"Climate change is the biggest single issue; it encompasses all the others," she says. "We have to keep active on environmental issues. You know, I don't even want to call them 'environmental.' The 'environment' is outside us, it's Out There. This whole thing is not Out There, it's a matter of issues of human health, of quality of life, of the very nature of human life. Being involved has made my life so rich. We're

Eelgrass protects and feeds the young of many marine animals, but it is declining in the world's oceans

all involved, every one of us, in an amazing opportunity to be involved in how our planet is shifting. I think it's an incredibly exciting time to be alive. And we need women in this work. Women have a perspective that leads to a more viable world, a world that is a sustainable place to live, that will be here for future generations."

Severn is the first to say that she has a great life. She has already done tremendous things for the environment, and she encourages the rest of us to do whatever we can to help. She couldn't have done what she has without the support of her parents and she encourages parents to support their children when they want to contribute.

Whatever else we may or may not be able to do, most people can protest to save a forest. We can help raise money, write letters, and make phone calls, and we can reduce, reuse, and recycle. Severn Cullis-Suzuki's life is about our planet and the life on it. She stays hopeful because she doesn't see any other way to go about her life and work. And, she says, "I go along with what the Dalai Lama says: If something's wrong and you can do something about it, do it. If you can't, forget it." She urges us and welcomes us all to take measures *now*, to act for the health of our planet and every living thing on it, so that today's children will have a world to live in.

Olya Melen

1980 -

Taking on a Government

"As a public-interest environmental lawyer, my goal is to seek the rule of law to preserve nature for present and future generations. Our fragile Mother Earth badly needs legal defenders."

Olya Melen made this statement in her acceptance speech for the 2006 Goldman Environmental Prize, the largest prize given to a grassroots environmentalist. A translator and a lawyer, she earned the award, a monetary prize equivalent to thirty-five years of her current salary, for her work to save the wetlands of the Danube Delta. She managed to stop the illegal

construction of a shipping canal from the Danube River into the Black Sea when she was just twenty-six years old.

A citizen of Ukraine, Olya was born when her country was part of the former Soviet Union, and she grew up as that union was coming apart. She went to university in Lviv, Ukraine, where she graduated with degrees in both translation and law.

As a member of the generation of young adults who lived under the system of government in former Soviet countries, Olya is familiar with that system and how it worked. In that way, she and her contemporaries are like the adults before them. But the older members of the environmental movement in Ukraine see a big difference in approach between their own generation and hers. People in her age group have never lived in terror of the local police or of the immensely powerful Soviet secret police, the KGB. So where their parents may have had strong opinions but were afraid to say anything, some members of Olya's generation have deeply held beliefs and are able to voice them. Olya Melen believes so passionately in the need to defend the earth and the life on it that when she was twenty-four years old she took the government of Ukraine to court.

In 2004, the government began a huge operation to dig up the delta of the Danube River to create a shipping link between the river and the Black Sea. Everyone agrees that this kind of link would bring huge financial benefits to that area of the world. But the government began to tear apart the delta wetlands without any real awareness of what it was doing. It did no study of the environmental impact of the canal route. There was no consultation with the people of the two countries most directly affected,

The average monthly salary in Ukraine is the equivalent of $220US. Environmental lawyers make the equivalent of about $300US a month.

Ukraine and Romania. And the interference with the wetlands broke international environmental law and agreements.

When this dredging up of the delta began, Olya realized what it meant. She had seen the area and knew its beauty and value. The first time she saw the delta wetlands, she was enchanted. “It looked like a miracle,” she says, “like an adventure to paradise.” More than a million acres of lakes and rivers form the delta, and they are beautiful and teeming with wildlife. For centuries, people have found it a magical place, and in that, Olya is no exception.

All over the world, wetlands are essential to the evolution and renewal of plant and animal life. Without them, the earth

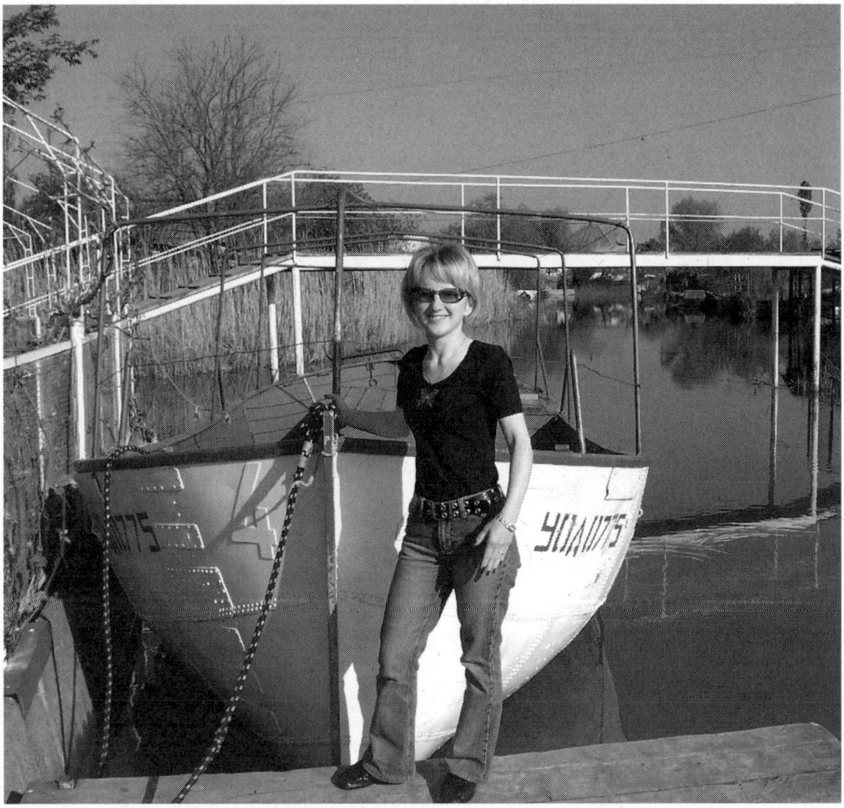

Olya Melen on the Danube River

could not sustain and replenish the millions of species that keep our environment healthy. Since many of the world's wetlands have already been destroyed, each one that remains is all the more important and necessary to the planet's health.

Large areas of reeds, known as reed beds, are necessary for the growth of young water creatures. These reed beds also clean the water and replenish the nutrients in it. The Danube Delta has the largest reed beds in the world. Because of them, the delta is one of the world's major breeding grounds for animals and plants. The United Nations considers the area so important that it has named the delta a UNESCO World Heritage Site and Biosphere Reserve. The Ramsar Convention is the only international environmental treaty dedicated to one kind of ecosystem: wetlands. Its 153 signing countries have designated the Danube Delta a Wetland of International Importance. It was into the richest part of this area that

Olya Melen, left, and two colleagues study a map of the Danube Delta

the government of Ukraine, against international agreements and without adequate ecological studies, public support, or even public knowledge, took huge dredging equipment and began to uproot and destroy this rich and ancient habitat.

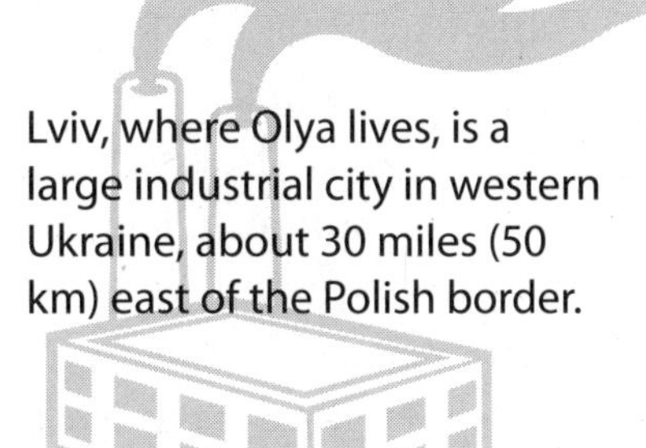

Lviv, where Olya lives, is a large industrial city in western Ukraine, about 30 miles (50 km) east of the Polish border.

The delta is at the eastern end of Ukraine. When the dredging began, Olya was living in Lviv, an industrial city in the western side of the country, about 30 miles (50 km) from the Polish border. She was working as a staff lawyer with Environmental-People-Law (EPL), one of the first grassroots environmental organizations set up in the former Soviet Union. Founded in 1994, EPL is, as the head of another major environmental organization in Ukraine states, "one of the most highly respected voices for citizen environmental rights in Europe and around the world." When environmentalists were afraid that nothing could be done to stop the destruction of the delta, Olya stepped up and volunteered to take the government of Ukraine to court. She offered to sue the government of her country in order to hold it accountable for its illegal and destructive actions, and to try to stop further disruption of the Delta.

She knew, she says, that many people thought she was crazy, or at least that what she was proposing to do was useless, insane, and possibly dangerous. Such an undertaking was unheard of, especially in a country that had been part of the Soviet Union. Public objection to government activity was an entirely new thing for Ukraine. Even more extraordinary was that anyone would actually try to stop the government from completing a project it had decided to carry out, and in fact had already started. Since Olya was twenty-four years old,

and this would be her first court case, her suggestion seemed outrageous. Ukrainian environmentalists would not stop her from trying, but they never dreamed that she could succeed. As for her opponents, they looked at the young, inexperienced woman and decided that she was no threat.

The people on both sides of the issue drastically underestimated Olya Melen. No one had any idea how informed, intelligent, and committed she was or how fierce she could be. They quickly found out.

Going into court for the first time, Olya was, as she said in an interview, “more than nervous — my hands were shaking, my voice was breaking, and it was really scary.” That was in 2004. In 2005, she went to court more than thirty times for this case. Usually she went alone or with one of her coworkers. Her opponents were older, experienced, and tough: “The government of Ukraine hired a lot of lawyers and they came to court all the time...sometimes three at a time, and they were quite aggressive.” But she quickly noticed that “being young was a good thing. Nobody expected to have a qualified opposing party in this suit. They all said, ‘She’s young, she knows nothing. She will not be able to convince the judge.’ So I caught them by surprise. The judges didn’t take me seriously at first, but then they decided that my arguments were quite sound. Then I was taken seriously.”

Not only was she taken seriously, many people saw her as dangerous. She was called a traitor. She was accused of being a spy. She received death threats. But Olya kept going. She had undertaken a cause that mattered, to herself, to many other people, to the delta, and to the planet. “I couldn’t let them down. I had to win.”

While the case was being heard, the “Orange Revolution” occurred in Ukraine. This peaceful upheaval took place after a corrupt election. The government that had declared itself elected was replaced by the government the people really had

elected. The new government pledged that it would rule by law. Since the destruction in the delta was the work of the previous government and was illegal, the new government's pledge was helpful to Olya's case. It also helped that Ukraine had applied for admission to the European Union (EU). Engaging in illegal and environmentally dangerous construction could harm that application (Ukraine did join the EU on January 1, 2007).

Olya Melen received the Goldman Environmental Prize in 2006

The case has reached a kind of conclusion — for now. The first phase of construction was completed, but the project has been stopped. Olya and other environmentalists do not argue that there should be no canal at all to connect the Danube and the Black Sea. If ships were able to make the trip down

the river and into the sea, it would help the economies of Ukraine, Romania, and several other countries. But the canal that was started goes through the richest and most important part of the wetland. Other routes are possible. And another route could meet the economic needs of several developing countries without destroying the wetlands. The president of Ukraine wants to see the canal built, but has not opposed the court decision. This is where things stand now. What will happen next remains to be seen.

Olya Melen still works with EPL. She has become the head of the organization's legal unit. She writes for the *Environmental Advocacy Journal* and is associated with Svitlana Kravchenko, the founder of EPL, who now trains environmental lawyers at the University of Oregon. Olya has been appointed a Fellow of the John Smith Memorial Trust in Britain. John Smith Fellows are young leaders from other nations who spend a year in Britain, observing how the British system is set up and how it works. She is not yet thirty, and already she has made huge contributions to the welfare of the earth. We will hear more, much more, from Olya Melen.

Glossary

Activist: a person who actively participates in a movement or organization, whose aim is to achieve a social or political goal; while there are many kinds of activists, the term is often used to refer to environmental, human rights, feminist, or ecological activists.

Biosphere: the part of the earth and its atmosphere that can support life; the living things on the earth and their environment.

DDT: dichloride diphenyl trichlorethane: an early insecticide spray once widely used, now banned in many places because of its poisonous effects on animals and humans; it is still manufactured and sent to developing nations; it helps in the control of the mosquito that spreads malaria, and is still legally used to control the disease.

Doctorate: see PhD.

Dredge: to dig up or deepen a river or channel using huge suction or digging machines.

Ecologist: a person who specializes in the study of ecology; ecologists are often also ecological activists.

Ecology: the study of the interrelationships among living things and their environment; the totality or pattern of the relationships of organisms and their environment.

Ecosystem: an ecological area or community and its environment, acting as a unit.

Environment: all the circumstances (soil, air, water, minerals, other living things) that surround an organism or group of organisms; these factors determine whether, and in what kind of health, the organism will survive.

Environmentalist: a person who works for the health and well-being of the global environment or of some part of that environment.

Ethology: the study of animal behavior, particularly in the wild.

Food chain: the order in an ecosystem in which one living thing eats another and is in turn eaten by another: a robin may eat a worm, and a fox may eat the robin. If one link in the chain is broken, that is, if one of the living things disappears, the balance in the chain is disturbed and all those above it may be in danger of starvation and another part of the chain may grow and further disrupt the balance. If all worms disappear, robins may starve and if they starve, foxes may starve. At the same time, the good that the worms do for the soil is removed and the soil becomes less rich and less able to support other life.

Goldman Prize: the largest prize granted to grassroots environmentalists; each year one person is chosen to receive the prize from each of six areas in the world.

Grassroots: people or groups getting together and acting from the local level rather than in large organizations or governments.

Habitat: the environment where an organism lives or where an organism would ordinarily be found.

Heavy metal: a metal of greater weight than most, particularly a poisonous metal like mercury or lead.

Indigenous peoples: Aboriginal peoples of any area.

NGO: non-governmental organization: a grassroots, not-for-profit group that works, usually internationally, for the benefit of some group of people or some part of the environment and is not connected to any government or large, international or multinational company.

Organism: any living being.

PCBs: polychlorinated biphenyl: industrial chemicals; these are environmental pollutants that gather in the living tissue of animals (including humans) and cause deformed babies and/or disease (often cancer).

PhD: Doctor of Philosophy: the most frequently granted of the doctorate degrees, the highest degree a person can earn in university; it involves courses, research, and a long research paper known as a thesis or dissertation; a person must ordinarily already have earned a bachelor's and master's degree.

Physicist: a scientist who specializes in physics, the study of matter, energy, and the relationships between them.

POPs: persistent organic pollutants: toxic chemicals that do not dissolve but collect in water and soil of the planet and then collect in the bodies of people and other living organisms, causing disease, malformation, or death; these chemicals include mercury, lead, DDT, and PCBs, among many others; they have collected in huge quantities all over the world, particularly in the North, far from where they originated.

Primate: any of the mammals who have developed hands and feet, a shortened snout, and an enlarged brain.

Right Livelihood Award: also called the Alternative Nobel Prize; Rachel Carson and Vandana Shiva have received the Right Livelihood Award.

Sustainable development: using resources in ways that do not destroy them or the ecosystem they are part of, but keep them alive and strong while they provide the material that is wanted from them; taking some sap from tree over a period of many years rather than cutting the trees down, for example, or cutting only some trees in any one area so that the other trees and the ecosystem of the area survive and continue to grow.

Resources

Rachel Carson

Breton, Mary Jo. *Women Pioneers for the Environment.* Boston: Northeastern University Press, 1998.

Burby, Liza N. *Rachel Carson: Writer and Environmentalist.* New York: PowerKids Press, 1997.

Carson, Rachel. *Silent Spring.* Boston and New York: Houghton Mifflin, 1962.

__. *The Sea Around Us.* Oxford and New York: Oxford, 1989.

__. *The Edge of the Sea.* Boston: Houghton Mifflin, 1955.

__. *The Sense of Wonder.* New York: Harper & Row, 1965. Original text 1956.

Freeman, Martha, ed. *Always, Rachel: The Letters of Rachel Carson and Dorothy Freeman, 1952-1964.* Boston: Beacon, 1995.

Greene, Carol. *Rachel Carson: Friend of Nature.* Danbury, CT: Grolier, 1992.

Wadsworth, Ginger. *Rachel Carson: Voice for the Earth.* Minneapolis: Lerner, 1992.

www.myhero.com/myhero/hero.asp?hero=rcarson

www.pbs.org/wgbh/aso/ontheedge/ecology/

www.pbs.org/wgbh/aso/databank/entries/btcars.html

www.rachelcarson.org

www.rachelcarsoncouncil.com

www.rachelcarsonhomestead.org

www.time.com/time/time100/scientist/profile/carson.html

Jane Goodall

Quotations are taken from Davies, www.nationalgeographic.com, and www.janegoodall.org
Davies, K. *Jane Goodall: A Researcher in Her Prime.* Associated Press, 1997.
Goodall, Jane. *Through a Window.* Boston: Houghton Mifflin, 1990.
__. *The Magic I Knew as a Child.* 1996.
Nichols, M. "Jane Goodall." *National Geographic,* December 1995:105-31.
www.myhero.com/myhero/hero.asp?hero=goodall_montvale
www.janegoodall.org/janegoodall
www.janegoodall.org/jan/gombe.asp
www.literati.net/Goodall
www.nationalgeographic.com/council/eir/bio_goodall.htm
www.wic.org/bio/jgoodall.htm
www.spirituallyfit.com/volume2/issue1/stories/janegoodall_1.htm

Dai Qing

Adams, Pat. Phone conversations with the author, January 10-12, 2007. Pat is on staff at Three Gorges Probe and Probe International.
Breton, Mary Jo. *Women Pioneers for the Environment.* Boston: Northeastern, 1998.
Qing, Dai. *Yangtze! Yangtze!* London and Toronto: Earthscan, 1994 (originally published in Chinese [sic] by Guizhou People's Publishing House, 1989).
www.businessweek.com
www.goldmanprize.org/node/155
www.multinationalmonitor.org/hyper/mm1297.06.html
www.pekingduck.org/archives/001617.php
www.probeinternational.org.tgp/index
www.threegorgesprobe.org/tgp/index.cfm?DSP=content&ContentID=918

Fatima Jibrell

Quotations come from the www.oxfam.org, www.hornrelief.com, and e-mails and conversation with Jim Lindsay.
Lindsay, Jim. E-mails with the author, December 2006 and January 2007.
__. Phone conversation with the author, January 13, 2007.
www.goldmanprize.org/node/113
hornrelief.8k.com/about.html
www.isna.net/services/horizons/current/EnvironmentalistHonored.htm
www.newscientist.com/article/mg17523506.100-female-intuition.html
www.oxfam.org/en/programs/development/hafrica/somalia_family.htm
tucacas.info/sunfirecooking/SFCnewweb/newsoctober2006/index.htm

Vandana Shiva

Breton, Mary Jo. *Women Pioneers for the Environment.* Boston: Northeastern University Press, 1998.
Shiva, Vandana. *Biopiracy: The Plunder of Nature and Knowledge.* Toronto: Between the Lines, 1997.
__. *Stolen Harvest: The Hijacking of the Global Food Supply.* Cambridge, MA: South End, 2000.
www.big-picture.tv/index.php?id=26&cat=&a=46
www.hinduonnet.com/2000/05/21/stories/3210414.htm
www.rightlivelihood.org/recip/v-shiva.html
uttarakhand.prayaga.org/threeheroes.html
www.yesmagazine.org/article.asp?ID=570.
Quotations are taken from this interview by Sarah Ruth van Gelder.

Sheila Watt-Cloutier

Watt-Cloutier, Sheila. "The Inuit Journey towards a POPs-Free World." In David Downie and Terry Fenge, eds.,

Northern Lights Against POPs. Montreal: McGill-Queen's University Press, 2003, 256-67.

__. "Don't Abandon Arctic to Climate Change." *The Globe and Mail*, May 24, 2006: A19.

www.inuitcircumpolar.com

www.nrtee-trnee.ca/eng/overview/Watt-Cloutier-Sheila_Bio_e.html

www.rollingstone.com/politics/story/8742369/the_emissary

www.sophieprize.org/Prize_winners/2005/index.html

www.thegreatwarming.com/localhero-interviewscloutier.htm

Sharon Beder

Beder, Sharon. *Power Play: The Fight to Control the World's Electricity*. Melbourne, Australia: Scribe; New York: The New Press, 2003; Korea: Kyobo Book Centre, 2005; Mexico: Fondo de Cultura Económica, 2005; Japan: Soshisha Ltd., 2006.

___. *Selling the Work Ethic: From Puritan Pulpit to Corporate PR.* London and New York: Zed Books, 2000; Melbourne: Scribe, 2000; Denmark: KLIM, 2004.

___. *Global Spin: The Corporate Assault on Environmentalism.* Devon, UK: Green Books, 1997, 2002; Melbourne: Scribe, 1997, 2000; White River Jct., VT: Chelsea Green, 1998, 2002; Osaka, Japan: Sogei Shuppan Publishing, 1999.

___. *The Nature of Sustainable Development*. Newham, Australia: Scribe, 1992, 1996.

__. E-mails with the author, October, November 2006, January 2007.

__. Phone conversations with the author, January 2007. Quotations are taken from these e-mails and conversations.

www.homepage.mac.com/herinst/sbeder/about.html

www.medialens.org/weblog/sharon_beder.php

www.ouw.edu.au/arts/staff/sbeder/index.html

www.wisenet-australia.org/profiles/beder.htm

Marina Silva

Hildebrandt, Ziporah. *Marina Silva: Defending Rainforest Communities in Brazil.* New York: Feminist Press, 2001.

www.goldmanprize.org/node/162

www.internacional.radiobras.gov.br/ingles/ministerios/environment_2004.php. Quotations are from this site.
ipsterraviva.net/tv/wsf2005/viewstory.asp?idnews=146
www.tierramerica.net/2003/0414/idialogos.shtml
www.thirdworldtraveler.com/Heroes/MarinaSilva.html
www.utexas.edu/opa/news/00newsreleases/nr_200003/nr_silva000323.html

Severn Cullis-Suzuki

Cullis-Suzuki, Severn. *Tell the World:A Young Environmentalist Speaks Out.* New York and Toronto: Doubleday, 1993. Includes her speech in Rio.
__. Phone interview with the author, November 20, 2006.
Quotations are from Severn's speech to the UN Summit and the telephone interview with the author.
__, et al., eds. *Notes from Canada's Young Activists: A Generation Speaks up for Change.* Vancouver: Greystone, 2007.
www.actioncanada.ca/english/2004.htm
www.earthfocus.org
www.skyfishproject.org
www.slothclub.org/pages/activity/japan/sevtour/sevspeech1992.htm
www.thegreatwarming.com
www.top20under20.ca/en/MentorProgram/scsuzuki.htm
www.unep.org
www.womennet.ca/directory.php?show&6479
www.yorku.ca/fes/changeyourworld/archive/keynote.asp
Contains the text of the speech to the UN Summit in Rio

Olya Melen

www.elan/org/custom/custompages/partnerDetail.asp
www.epl.org/ua
www.goldmanprize.org/node/143 (with video)
www.goldmanprize.org/node/205
greenhorizon.rec.org/insight/green-torchbearer-for-an-orange-revolution.html/

greenhorizon.rec.org/about-us.html
www.grist.org/news/maindish
Nijhuis, Michelle. "The Blew Danube." Interview with Olya Melen, available online at www.grist.org/news/maindish/2006/04/25/nijhuis-melen
www.johnsmithmemorialtrust.org/web/site/Articles&News/Olya_Melen.Prize.asp
www.law.uoregon.edu/org/enr/skravchenko.htm
www.ramsar.org/index_about_ramsar_htm
WHC.UNESCO.ORG/en/list

Photo Credits

Rachel Carson

Page 5: © U.S. Fish and Wildlife Service
Page 6: © Rachel Carson Council/www.rachelcarsoncouncil.com
Page 10: © U.S. Fish and Wildlife Service
Page 13: © U.S. Fish and Wildlife Service

Jane Goodall

Page 17: © Danita Delimont/Alamy
Page 23: © Bruce Coleman Inc./Alamy

Dai Qing

Page 27: courtesy The Goldman Environmental Prize
Page 30: courtesy NASA
Page 31: Wikimedia Commons/Nowozin

Fatima Jibrell

All photos courtesy Fatima Jibrell/James Lindsay/
www.sunfirecooking.com

Vandana Shiva

Page 45: © Linda Wolf/www.lindawolf.net
Page 51: Wikimedia Commons/Elke Wetzig

Sheila Watt-Cloutier

All photos courtesy Sheila Watt-Cloutier

Sharon Beder

All photos courtesy Sharon Beder

Marina Silva

All photos courtesy The Goldman Environmental Prize

Severn Cullis-Suzuki

Page 79: © Green Toronto Awards
Page 86: (top) Wikimedia Commons/Nick Wiebe (bottom) © Green Toronto Awards
Page 88: Public domain/Colin Faulkingham

Olya Melen

All photos courtesy The Goldman Environmental Prize

More from The Women's Hall of Fame series

"A must for the junior high and high school library." — *Kliatt*

- Ages 9-13
- Paperback with black and white photos
- $10.95

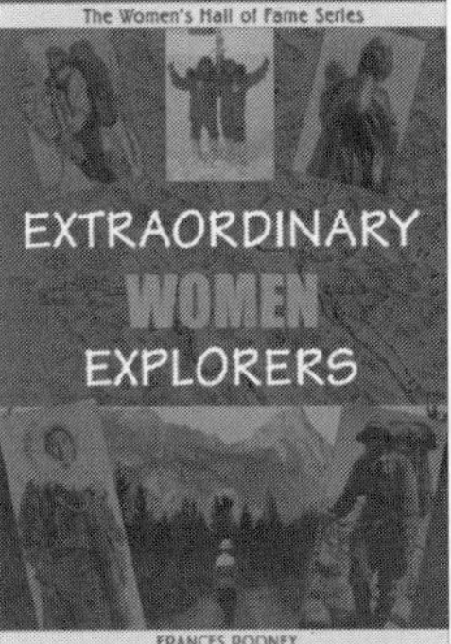

Exceptional Women Environmentalists
Frances Rooney
ISBN: 978-1-897187-22-7

Astonishing Women Artists
Heather Ball
ISBN: 978-1-897187-23-4

Incredible Women Inventors
Sandra Braun
ISBN: 978-1-897187-15-9

Remarkable Women Writers
Heather Ball
ISBN: 978-1-897187-08-1

Magnificent Women in Music
Heather Ball
ISBN: 978-1-897187-02-9

Extraordinary Women Explorers
Frances Rooney
ISBN: 978-1-896764-98-6

Spectacular Women in Space
Sonia Gueldenpfennig
ISBN: 978-1-896764-88-7

Super Women in Science
Kelly Di Domenico
ISBN: 978-1-896764-66-5

Great Women Leaders
Heather Ball
ISBN: 978-1-896764-81-8

Amazing Women Athletes
Jill Bryant
ISBN: 978-1-896764-44-3

Fabulous Female Physicians
Sharon Kirsh with Florence Kirsh
ISBN: 978-1-896764-43-6